MW00885748

Queens of the Court

Pam Greer

Published by Lechner Syndications

www.lechnersyndications.com

Copyright © 2014 Pam Greer

All rights reserved. No part of this book may be reproduced or transmitted in any form
or by any means, electronic or mechanical, including photocopying, recording, or by any
information storage and retrieval system, without written permission from the
publisher. For more information contact Lechner Syndications, 2337 Heron Street,
Victoria, British Columbia V8R 5Z7

ISBN 13: 978-1-927794-19-7

"A good team can win a volleyball game when they are ahead, but only a great team can win when they are behind."

~Anonymous

.

CONTENTS

CHAPTER 1

"Your hands are a weapon," Coach Mike proclaimed to the new recruits, holding a volleyball high in the air. "If you want Hickory Academy to achieve the same success as last year, and if you want to take that success and go even farther, then you've got to use that weapon with an invincible accuracy and force." He slammed the volleyball across the net so hard, it looked as if it lost a significant amount of air when it crashed into the ground. "Welcome to my army, ladies."

Payton Moore beamed, feeling a fluster of anticipation in her heart. The start of any new season always brought with it an enormous amount of hope, no matter the sport, but today Payton had an extra dose of anxious energy zipping through her, especially after the way the Hickory Academy volleyball team performed last season.

Headed by Coach Mike Ross, the volleyball program at Hickory Academy was fairly new. Where most schools had decades' worth of trophies and medals in their display cases, their volleyball team was only in its fourth year. They were newbies, yet the varsity team had managed to win Regionals last year and just barely lost out in the Sub-State Tournament. It'd been a season full of highs and lows, but they'd pulled through in the end, taking home the District and Regional Tournament trophies.

And this year, we'll bring home the State trophy, Payton predicted to

1

herself.

She looked around at the team she hoped would get them there. Having lost a bulk of their strong players to graduation, including their star *libero*, Annette, the volleyball team's doors had once again been left wide open. There were no try-outs. Those who were interested simply had to show up today to their first official practice. Most of them had gone to volleyball camp together, but there were a few girls Payton didn't recognize, mostly freshmen.

Earlier, before Coach Mike had started his opening speech, Payton had watched the girls file into the gymnasium. It was obvious their success the previous year had drawn a lot more girls out than in past seasons, but not as many as Payton would have thought. There were more familiar faces than there were new. In many ways, this was an advantage, because the coaches knew the type of talent they had to work with, but it also meant they might not be able to fill the void of the seniors who had graduated.

The loudest of the incoming freshmen was Valerie Sutton. With her shiny auburn hair, light blue eyes, and ability to charm the moodiest of the moodiest, she was already growing popular among the other girls on the team. Payton knew her from basketball. Val was a year younger, but they had played on the same team in middle school and had spent a week at basketball camp together earlier in the summer. Payton was excited to have Val on the team. She was a top athlete and ambitious, traits Payton admired, and though not a close friend, Payton did consider her an awesome teammate. She looked forward to getting to know Val better.

"...and if you want to win hard, you have to sweat hard," Coach Mike continued, still in the middle of his speech. "If you miss a practice, you better have a darn good reason. Did ya hear that, ladies? I want commitment, not excuses..."

After more talk about how hard work was the only path to success, he dismissed the girls temporarily to stretch on their own as he and his assistant, Coach Gina Williams, spoke quietly to each other in the corner of the gymnasium, no doubt planning the type of drills they were going to throw at the girls to test their skills.

Again, the anticipation of a new season made Payton's heart skip a beat. She hadn't done as well as she would have liked to last year, her talents on the court coming up short, unlike basketball where she was a slam dunk queen, thanks to her height. But after the basketball season had come to an end, she'd spent a majority of her time practicing her volleyball skills with her dad. This year, she was a sophomore, and she was marching into the season older, wiser, and stronger. She was prepared or, at least, as prepared as she could be. She still had a little ways to go before she dominated the volleyball court the way she did the basketball court.

Payton looked over at Neeka Leigh, her bestie, watching as Neeka clipped her short brown spirals away from her dark, dignified face. "Ready for another season?" Payton asked.

Neeka nodded, looking fierce. "Let's do this!"

Unlike her, Neeka was a pro at volleyball, surpassing her in almost every way possible. It'd been a surprise to them both last year, given that Neeka spent most of her time on the bench in basketball. She'd only signed up for volleyball at Payton's insistence when, after witnessing Payton's athleticism, the varsity volleyball girls had recruited Payton onto their team.

Originally, Neeka had been assigned to JV, having never played volleyball before. Back then, the varsity girls had barely acknowledged her existence. But once Neeka had started shining on the court, she'd quickly been promoted to Coach Mike's starting line-up.

"The surprise of the season," Coach Mike had said, speaking of Neeka at their end of season party when he'd presented her with the Best Leader award. Most Valuable Player had gone to Annette, their captain. Payton had walked home with Most Improved Player.

Payton felt a playful tug on the back of her messy ponytail. She turned, happy to see Lacey Knox, a senior, standing behind her. Of all the upperclassmen, Lacey was by far the friendliest. Last year, when the rest of the girls on the varsity team had started ignoring Payton due to her bad performance, Lacey had been the only one to offer her some solace.

"Time for Round Two," Lacey chirped. "I hope all y'all have been practicing, because this season we're gonna smoke the competition like they were taters roasting on my nana's fire pit."

"Watch out Nashville!" Neeka exclaimed.

"Girl, forget Nashville. I was talking about Tennessee!" Lacey's blue eyes sparkled against her tan skin. Though her eyes and hair were fair, Lacey was half Latina. But a bit of a tomboy, she was shy about her beauty.

"Woo woo! State, here we come!" Payton said, waving her arms in the air.

Lacey clapped her hands. "Did you hear? That new company selling the miracle water stuff is one of the State sponsors. They paid some big cheddar for extra TV coverage."

"What does that mean?" Payton asked.

Stretching out her arm, Neeka answered. "It means that the final of the State Tournament will likely air on a big network."

"Cool!"

"Can you spritz some of that miracle water on me now," Neeka moaned, dropping her arm. "After fifteen summers on this planet, you'd think I'd be used to the August heat. Not yet."

"At least we're indoors," Lacey said. "In fact, with that luxury, I'm surprised volleyball isn't more popular. I feel bad for the cross country girls out running laps on the track."

"Shhh," Payton hushed. "You don't want Coach Mike getting any ideas. He'll say it builds character." She lowered her voice at the end of the last sentence so that it sounded deep and hoarse. "Character turns strong players into champions."

"Ummm... Were you trying to sound like Batman?" Neeka asked. A hint of the giggles made her lips quiver.

"No! I was an army sergeant," Payton objected.

"I'm sorry, but that was definitely Batman," Lacey insisted.

Amused, Payton tried again. "I am Payton Moore," she said in the same deep growl.

"I am Renika Leigh," Neeka echoed.

They turned to Lacey expectantly. "I am Lacey Knox?" the senior squeaked.

The three girls burst into giggles, but their laughter was short lived as Coach Mike commanded them to line up for drills.

Game time.

Lacey left them so she could help lead the drills. As a senior, she was definitely on the varsity team this year. Regulations said all seniors had to be. But everyone else had to earn their spot on the team. Though there were no try-outs in general for volleyball this year, the girls were competing among themselves for a varsity position. The underdogs last year, Hickory Academy now had a reputation among the district that they wanted to live up to. They were the defending Regional Champions and now one of the favorites to play at State. Only the best among them would wear a varsity jersey.

As they formed a line near the net, Payton listened as some of the girls talked nervously among themselves. The freshmen especially were unsure of what to expect. From what she could hear, Val was the only freshman with any real experience. As the Hickory Academy middle school didn't have a volleyball program, Val had attended a few of the high school JV practices the previous year, which were hosted in the middle school gym while varsity took over the high school gym. But she'd never been allowed to play in any of the matches.

Coach Mike and Coach Gina had highlighted Val's efforts in their petition to introduce a volleyball program to the middle school, hoping it would cultivate experienced players early on, before the high school level, but the Board of Directors had cited budget restraints and dismissed the petition.

So now it's up to Team Scary Pancake to help the freshmen girls, Payton thought.

Payton, Neeka, and their friend Selina Cho had a pretty good idea where they stood in the eyes of the coaches. During the summer, Coach Mike had called them into his office, along with the seniors, to strategize for the upcoming season. Mostly, the three underclassmen would resume the same roles they had as freshmen. Neeka would start with varsity while Payton and Selina would be substitutes. All three would start for JV to fill in the gaps their lack of numbers created.

The main difference this year, besides Coach Mike expecting them to be leaders, especially among the younger girls, was that Payton would primarily practice with JV.

It was a bit of a blow when she found out. Last year, she'd been recruited onto the varsity volleyball team to be their star athlete, and now she was being forced back to concentrate on JV. She had hoped her JV days were over.

But Coach Gina had summed it up nicely, putting her usual soft touch on Coach Mike's more robust authority. As the assistant coach, Coach Gina was in charge of the JV girls. She explained to Payton that it was in the interest of longevity for Payton to focus on the JV team. Many of the freshmen girls would be in the same position Payton had been last year—eager to play but lacking the necessary skills. Both coaches thought Payton could give them the inspiration they needed to find their own talents within, making them stronger so that when the varsity girls graduated, they had well-rounded players to fill their positions.

"It means the varsity team can live up to its new reputation for quite a few years down the road," Coach Gina had said eagerly. "That makes you are not only central to the Hickory Academy volleyball program this year, but also to its future. But don't worry, your jump serve is too good for varsity to let go of. You'll still substitute at varsity matches."

After hearing her words, Payton had managed a smile. "Well, when you put it like that…"

After the meeting, she and Neeka had invited Selina over for a sleepover. Together, they came up with Team Scary Pancake. She would like to credit the name to the move in volleyball known as a pancake, when a player dived to the ground and spread their hand out flat so the ball could bounce off it. It was a pretty scary move, Payton thought. But the name had truly come from the gooey, clumpy, inedible pancakes the girls had tried to make the next morning. As they threw the batter down the sink, they made a pact that they would try to keep JV and varsity united, starting by working one-on-one with any freshmen who joined to make sure they felt wanted and part of the team.

Coach Mike's booming voice interrupted Payton's thoughts and the chatter from the rest of the girls. "We're going to start with a basic drill called peppering. If you don't know what peppering is, you might as well head over to the JV side now."

Two of the freshmen who had missed summer camp walked over to where Coach Gina was standing, their faces red but resilient.

"At least they're not walking out the door," Neeka whispered to Payton.

Though nearing her forties, Coach Gina jumped up and down. "Two new recruits," she sang joyfully.

"Not yet," Payton whispered back. "But we forgot to warn them to beware of the cheerleader."

As soon as the words left Payton's mouth, she regretted them. Coach Gina was known to be a bit too enthusiastic at times, but the woman was fair and compassionate, her words soothing compared to Coach Mike's rawness. And she was a killer player, having been the star of her college volleyball team. Payton respected that, hoping for the same in terms of basketball when she graduated and started college a few years down the line.

"Now, for the rest of you, I hope you were practicing in the off season, because I'm not going to show any mercy," Coach Mike warned. "If you want to be standing on the podium when we reclaim our title as Regional Champions, then you better be willing to work for it."

Unexpectedly, the doors to the gymnasium were thrown open, creating a loud bang that echoed around Coach Mike's words.

A girl with dark brown skin and colorful pieces of yarn weaved into her black cornrows burst into practice. She was beautiful, with deep, round eyes the color of ground coffee and a heart-shaped face. Though she was obviously panicked, she held her composure with the grace of a ballerina fluttering toward the stage.

"I'm sorry I'm late," she gasped, moving quickly to the back of the drill line.

"What's your name?" Coach Mike asked, not at all impressed with her tardiness.

The girl stepped forward, an unbreakable confidence about her. "My name is Courtney Adams, sir. I just transferred here from California, though my parents are Southerners through and through."

Coach Mike frowned. "You're not on my list."

"The lady at the registrar said I just had to attend the first practice," Courtney stated, not at all shy. "I only officially registered for Hickory Academy this morning. That's why I'm late."

Satisfied with the explanation, Coach Mike scribbled her name onto his clipboard. "Have you played volleyball before?"

"Yes. In middle school. I'm a freshman this year."

"And what position did you play?"

Courtney hesitated, choosing her words wisely. "To be totally honest, sir, I was the best hitter on my team."

Hitter? Payton swallowed, her insecurities from last year returning. A hitter herself, she had enough competition as it was with Selina and the other varsity girls. Any more competition and she could find herself sitting on the JV bench as well as the varsity one.

"Well, well," Coach Mike said, pleased by Courtney's confident attitude. "Looks like we have someone new to keep you girls on your toes."

CHAPTER 2

"Remember, Team Scary Pancake!" Selina Cho yelled from across the gymnasium, winking at Payton as the girls partnered off for the peppering drill. As usual, Selina's delicate Asian features were scrunched into a hard look of determination. "We don't need any more Annette's around!"

Annette, their previous captain, had been bowed up most of the season, her smile only appearing when they were on a winning streak. Her tendency to shout out threats and shut players out when they weren't performing well led to mass division within the team, resulting in each player's main concern being herself instead of the game. They had still played well, but it was only after the girls had reconnected and started working together as one that they really began to excel.

Though the freshmen were new, they were an important part of Team Scary Pancake's plan to keep the Hickory Academy volleyball team on the top podium. One day, the freshmen would be seniors. Everything they learned throughout the years would shape the leaders they would become. Payton wanted to set a good example for the girls so that they understood the importance of teamwork. In volleyball, when a team was only allowed three moves to send the ball over the net, teamwork was everything. Team Scary Pancake had decided that the best way to help the freshmen grow into not only good players, but great teammates, was to work with them directly.

9

Payton watched as Selina, her eyes set like steel, marched her way over to the two girls who didn't know what peppering was.

Easy, Payton advised silently, sending her thoughts toward Selina. *You don't want to frighten them away*. Selina had a good heart, but the girl was as tough as cow leather. She could be intimidating, especially with the heavy make-up she wore around her eyes.

Looking around at who was left, Payton spotted Val over by the drinking fountain. Perfect. She'd been fixin' to work with Val. Like Payton, Val was naturally athletic. In basketball, she wasn't the best girl on the team, but she was good. She moved fast and was persistent. Though they didn't talk much outside the court, they'd played well together at basketball camp. Payton was sure it'd be the same for volleyball.

"Hey, want to partner up?" she asked.

Val took a last sip of water from the fountain then turned, looking Payton up and down before switching on a bright smile. "Sure," she said enthusiastically. "Just give me One Moore Minute while I grab something from my bag."

One Moore Minute.

Payton blushed. Val was quoting the chant the student body had used at their tournament matches when Payton had unleashed her jump serve. To date, she was the only girl in the district who could successfully carry out a topspin jump serve—one that allowed her to hit almost anywhere across the net, especially where the other team had a hard time receiving it.

She hadn't always been a celebrated member of the team. Far from it. She had used to be a laughing stock at their matches, fumbling around like a cat on wheels. It was only when her Biology teacher, Mr. B, had encouraged her to specialize a skill, one that correlated with her natural abilities, that Payton discovered what an epic server she could be. Now, she was known across the district for her jump serve.

This year, I won't give anyone a chance to laugh at me, Payton vowed as she followed Val to the bleachers.

She was a little surprised Val was taking her time. Around them, the rest of the girls were busy with the drill, trying to show off their skills to Coach Mike, hoping for a spot on varsity, notably the sophomores and juniors.

Near to her, Selina instructed the two new freshmen, now officially on the JV team, on what to do.

"The peppering drill is pretty simple. You pass the ball back and forth to each other in a particular order—set, pass, hit. First, when you set the ball," she formed a triangle with her thumbs and fingers just above her forehead, "you shape your hands into a triangle like this. Then you push your arms up and forward, above your head, sending the ball into the air."

The girls imitated her movements while the ball stayed safely on the ground, untouched while they learned.

Selina continued. "Next, to pass the ball, or bump it as we say, you extend your arms out in front of you and fold your hands together. Keeping your arms straight, you want the ball to land somewhere in the middle of your forearm."

"I remember this from PE class," one of the girls declared. "It's called a platform."

"Exactly," Selina said. "Remember, when you pass, you use your legs for force. Now, lastly, to hit the ball, you take a flat hand and use the bottom of your palm to make contact with the ball. We call this spiking." She demonstrated the motion by hitting her dominant hand against the closed fist of her other hand. "And that's the peppering drill. Set. Pass. Hit."

Payton was awestruck. Selina looked so self-assured and polished as she instructed the girls. Her friend had been a pretty decent player last year, but now she was improving rapidly. And it showed, even in the way she stood with a straight posture, like a professional who really knew what she was doing. Payton wished she carried the same confidence. Though she was a far cry from the stumbling mess she had been before, she knew as she watched Selina that she still had a far way to go.

Turning back to the bleachers, she was suddenly relieved Val wouldn't require much instruction, just a few pointers regarding her technique.

From her bag, Val pulled out a plum purple volleyball. "Do you mind if we use this one? It's my lucky ball. I've been using it *all year* to practice."

For some reason, her words had the same intensity as a threat, but Payton shook the thought away. Val was ambitious, that was true. But she wasn't Annette. She didn't make things personal.

"I have a lucky volleyball at home too. I stuck Titans stickers all over it," Payton said, referring to Tennessee's football team. "But I'm not sure we're allowed to bring our own balls to practice."

Valerie laughed. "Don't be silly. Coach Gina won't mind."

"Yeah, but Coach Mike is the one you really need to impress."

Val thought about it for a moment. "You know what, you're right." She immediately put the ball back into her gym bag.

After grabbing a fresh ball from the hammock-style stand near the net, Payton led Valerie to an empty space. Building a rhythm, they passed to the ball to each other with ease. It was a wonder what a year's difference could make. This time last year, Payton kept angling her arms awkwardly as she learned the exact same drill with Lacey and Annette.

Remembering Team Scary Pancake's mission to make the freshmen feel like part of the team, Payton said to Val, "You're really quite good. I knew you attended a few practices with JV last year. It'll be nice to finally have you playing in the matches with us."

Val's face lit up. She was obviously pleased by the compliment. "It's so different from basketball, isn't it?"

"Yeah, surprisingly so."

"I mean, in basketball, you're a legend. I say you'll definitely be on varsity this year, now that you're no longer a freshman. But volleyball... Well, you're just the same as all of us. Except for that amazing jump serve you have. That's incredible."

"Thanks!" Payton said. "I worked hard to perfect that jump serve."

"So what's your role on the team this year? Do you know yet?"

Payton knew, but there was no way she was going to tell Val she'd been slightly demoted to mostly JV, not until the teams were officially assigned. "I'm assuming it'll be a lot like last year. I'll play JV and varsity. And what about you? What position do you hope to play?"

Please don't say hitter, Payton prayed.

"Actually, I was hoping to be *libero* this year."

The admission surprised Payton, but it made sense. Val was never one to let a few bumps and bruises get in her way. The *libero* was the main person responsible for passing the ball on to the setter or, at the very least, keeping the ball in play. Sometimes it meant diving on hands and knees to prevent the ball from touching the ground after an attack. It was an important role. With unlimited substitutions, a *libero* could replace any player in the back line.

"Well, with Annette graduated, you have a good chance," Payton remarked. "What made you want to be a *libero*?"

"You know. The ability to take the place of any player. I like having that power."

Across the gym, Coach Gina praised Selina with a high-pitched squeal, grabbing everyone's attention. "You're simply the best," she gushed. "Well done for taking the initiative to teach these girls. You're a superstar, Selina."

Val grumbled something under her breath. Payton didn't catch what she said, but it was probably in line with what everyone was thinking. Sometimes, Coach Gina's enthusiasm could be a bit overdone. It wasn't good for a player's concentration. Too much spirit, and you'd be sucked into an ego tornado.

Unexpectedly, Val yelled for Courtney, who was halfway down the court. "Hey, California, think you can hit this?"

Val served the ball. It went flying toward Courtney, who, watching the ball travel, positioned herself so that she had just enough time to jump in the air and slam the ball back. It wasn't a perfect hit; it was forceful, but her aim was off. Instead of returning the ball to Val, it landed just at Payton's feet. Still, the stunt was enough to have Coach Gina clapping.

"Girls, that was fantastic! I'm so impressed," she cheered. The woman looked as if she was ready to do a toe touch.

"It was messy," Coach Mike barked. "Next time you girls want to show off, make sure you have something worth delivering."

Dropping her eyes to the floor, Val silently returned to the peppering drill with Payton.

"Don't worry," Payton reassured her. "He's always like that."

"I can handle it," Val said defensively.

Some part in the back of Payton's mind answered, *I'm sure you can.*

****

At the end of practice, the girls were told to change back into their clothes and then return to the gymnasium bleachers for a final verdict on who would play on the JV and varsity teams. Payton wasn't worried. She already knew what to expect. But she hoped Coach Mike didn't formally announce to everyone that she would no longer be practicing with the varsity team, but would instead spend her afternoons in the middle school gym with JV.

When Payton returned to the gym, wearing an oversize Titans jersey and cut-off shorts, neither of the coaches could be seen. She sat near Neeka near the top row and waited with the rest of the girls. Neeka was on her phone, presumably with her brother Jamari by the cross look on her face. While Payton waited for Neeka to hang up, she once again listened to the conversations floating around her.

"Varsity needs a *libero*. I'm sure I'll make the team," Val calculated, speaking with the girl next to her.

"Will they put freshmen on varsity?" the girl asked.

"They did last year. Look at how well Neeka turned out. I'm sure they're open to it, anyway."

Val then whispered something inaudible to the girl. Whatever it was, the girl burst out into laughter.

"You're so bad," she hissed.

Neeka's voice suddenly rose. "I don't care if you're a big hairy senior now," she said into the phone. "Ma is paying you twenty dollars a week in gas money to take me to practices. You better be here in ten minutes to take Payton and me home, or I'm gonna blast Papa's awful polka CD so loud in your jeep, the whole town will hear. You'll never be able to show your face in school again." There was a pause. "Yes! I said polka CD!"

Frustrated, she hung up the phone. "The school year hasn't even started yet, and already his big fat head has senioritis. Brothers!" she huffed.

"Tell me about it," Courtney said, sitting next to them. "I have five. All younger. It's like totes mania in our house all the time."

Unusual for her character, Neeka suddenly seemed shy. Payton understood. Courtney was stunning. She could easily be a teen model.

"I like your cornrows. They're very Bohemian," Neeka commented.

Courtney smiled. "I could easily turn your spirals into cornrows, if you want."

Neeka shook her head. "Ma would never allow it. It's too hippy for her taste."

"What about you, Payton?" Courtney asked. "Your hair is a bit mousy, if you don't mind me saying so. Let's glam it up with some cornrows. I'll sew some blue and white thread in—Titans colors."

Payton thought of how much it would freak her mom out. Allison Moore was very similar to Neeka's mom when it came to fashion and modesty. She would consider cornrows too wild for her fifteen-year-old daughter. Her dad, Brandon Moore, would probably think the same, even with Titans colors sewn in. But he was living in Cincinnati now, so it wasn't as though he could stop her.

"I might just take you up on that," she decided keenly. "Perhaps when the volleyball and basketball seasons are over."

"Zowzers," Neeka said, looking at Payton in astonishment. "Quiet Payton turns teen rebel."

Payton stuck her tongue out. "I'm a quiet outcast with mad v-ball skills. Of course I'm a secret rebel."

"That must be why George likes you so much." Neeka grinned.

George was their friend Rose's cousin, who also attended Hickory Academy. Ever since the Biology class they had shared, George had been asking Payton to the school's various dances. But Payton wasn't interested. After recovering from her crush on Mr. B last year, the only boy who currently caught her attention was Torin Yater-Wallace, the famous teen freestyle skier. He was hot!

Using the public entrance, Coach Mike and Coach Gina swiftly walked back into the gymnasium, likely coming from Coach Mike's office.

"You did a wonderful job today, y'all," Coach Gina began as the girls grew quiet. "Those of you who are placed on JV with me, don't be too disheartened. Think of it as varsity-in-training. We'll have loads of fun while we train you up."

Coach Mike took over. "Now that our numbers are up a margin, we don't have to switch players between JV and varsity as often," he announced. "The three girls who played for both JV and varsity last year will continue to do so, but the rest of you will remain on the team you're assigned today, unless you suddenly demonstrate some super power."

Payton noticed Courtney tense in anticipation. Having played for her middle school, she was probably hoping she'd be placed on varsity, since she had more experience than any of the other freshmen here. It must be hard, Payton thought, leaving a team behind and not knowing how the new school would receive you.

"Seniors aren't allowed to play JV. Since we didn't hold try-outs this year, all seniors automatically are placed on varsity," Coach Mike continued.

They all had expected as much.

"Similarly, so that we can ensure your talents are nourished properly, all freshmen are automatically assigned JV this year. Unless, again, you have some hidden super power."

"Call me Wonder Woman," Val said. She looked disappointed at the news, as did Courtney.

Coach Gina then read out the remaining girls who would join JV, followed by Coach Mike listing the girls who had made varsity. It was clear experience had been a key factor in their decision-making. Every girl on varsity had played for Hickory Academy before.

"Buck up," Val said to the other freshmen girls when the coaches were finished. "Look how far Payton has come. She's an inspiration. If she can keep her place on varsity, then next year any of us can make it."

It sounded like praise to Payton, but Neeka didn't hear it that way. "And what the pajamas is that supposed to mean, freshman?" she demanded.

Val laughed it off. "Payton knows how much I love her. It was a compliment. We're basketball sisters, remember?"

Neeka relaxed. "Just remember, we're all a team. We may be divided between JV and varsity, but we all represent the volleyball program here at Hickory Academy. It's all of us against all of them." Authority and passion filled Neeka's voice as she spoke.

Payton watch in admiration as her friend took charge. Neeka had really blossomed, grown from a pea to a princess. Payton had no doubt that, under Neeka's leadership, Hickory Academy volleyball was going to rumble like a lightning storm all the way to State.

CHAPTER 3

Sophomore year.

Neeka leaned against her locker, taking it all in. Located near the downtown area of Nashville, Hickory Academy had a lot of history in the city. It was visible in the old wooden panels that lined the grand hallway and the 1920s-style marble floors. The central part of the building had been around for nearly a hundred years, but numerous extensions had been added onto the school since then, giving the rest of the building a more modern look. Now, there had been talk of building a top-of-the-line music center ever since the son of some famous country singer had started attending.

Looking around, Neeka giggled to herself. Though elegant, the expensive decor of the grand hallway hadn't stopped the students from throwing loads of glitter-filled signs and colorful cut-outs around the place. Across from her, there was a poster of a grumpy-looking cat with the caption, "Can't take a good Instagram? Join the photography club and learn how to take the perfect selfie!"

I can't believe this is my second year in high school, Neeka thought.

Freshman year had been thrilling but also a little terrifying. Middle school had been an easy transition from elementary school; they were pretty much just treated like little kids who had experienced a growth spurt. But high school—things were different. There were more responsibilities. More rules. More expectations. There was more homework. She'd be driving soon. Yikes! The idea of sitting behind the wheel blew her mind.

But mostly, in high school, there was more pressure to fit in. The benefit of a private school like Hickory Academy was that their school uniforms—a long plaid skirt, polo shirt, and blazer for the girls—meant she didn't have to worry about being judged based on what type of clothes she wore. She was thankful for that. But most of the kids at Hickory Academy were wealthy, whereas she was here based purely on a scholarship.

Money had meant very little when they were younger, but now... When the time came, how would she explain her used car when most of her classmates had shiny new ones? Or that she had to stick to fast food over fancy restaurants on a Friday night? Or that her prom dress wouldn't be designer? Her parents were far from poor; they were quite comfortable, but GAP clothes looked like they came from a thrift store compared to some of the purses and jewelry her classmates had.

So though sophomore year was a lot less intimidating than freshman year, it carried with it a whole new basket of worries.

Neeka sighed against the cool metal of her locker, then decided there was no point worrying about it. She fitted in with most people. There was no reason that should change now just because her wallet was a little thinner than those of her classmates.

The crowd of students around her abruptly broke apart as a body came hurling through them. With a huge smile on her face, Payton pushed past her classmates toward Neeka. She couldn't be missed. Having grown even taller over the summer, she towered above the others.

"Did you see what the cheer squad did to Big Joe?" Payton asked excitedly when she reached Neeka's locker.

Neeka quickly opened her locker and shoved her books inside. As she did, her copy of *Diary of a Young Volleyball Star* slipped out, bouncing off Payton's toe before it hit the ground.

"You still reading this?" Payton asked as she picked it up. "I really don't think Coach Gina wrote it."

"Well, I do," Neeka said, snatching the book back. "And even if

19

she didn't, it has some really good advice in it on how to lead a team."

Toward the end of the summer, while rifling through the volleyball books at the city library, Neeka had come across *Diary of a Young Volleyball Star*, written by Regina Solis. The book was a series of diary entries of a girl as she transitioned from her final year of high school volleyball to her years playing for a top college team.

It fit Coach Gina's own personal history perfectly. Coach Gina been a minor celebrity in the volleyball world during her college years. She'd even gone pro for a short while afterward, before deciding to settle down in Nashville with her husband, tired of all the traveling. And though she was known as Coach Gina Williams, it was her married name. No one knew her maiden name, the one she had before she was married. But Neeka had noticed that she always wore a gold necklace of a sun around her neck during practice. Solis, in Spanish, meant sun.

She was certain Regina Solis was now Gina Williams.

After finding the book in the library, she'd immediately showed it to Payton, but Payton wasn't convinced.

"Coach Gina doesn't look Spanish," Payton had said. "She has blue peepers."

"Yeah, but she also has black curly hair. Look at Lacey. She's half Latina, and she has blonde hair and blue eyes. The name could come from Coach Gina's grandfather or father. At camp, wasn't she talking about her recent vacation to *Barcelona*? Maybe she was visiting family in Spain. Geesh, Payton, we learned all about genetics last year in Mr. B's class. You know you can't base hereditary lineage on looks alone."

Payton threw her hands up in surrender. "Okay, okay. No need for big words. I gotcha. But I still don't think it's her. Is there an author photo?"

"No," Neeka admitted. "I'm afraid not."

After their conversation, Payton had lost interest, but Neeka couldn't put the book down. When it came time to return it to the library, she'd begged her ma to order it online. It was no longer in print, so the copy Neeka received was used. Whoever owned the book before her had left lipstick stains and stickers of nineties boy bands all over the pages, but Neeka didn't mind. As long as she could read the diary entries, that was all she cared about. She didn't show it to anyone else, in case Coach Gina had kept it a secret on purpose.

"So... Big Joe?" Payton asked, drawing Neeka away from her locker. "Have you seen him?"

"No. What's up with the J-man?" she asked, intrigued as they walked toward the cafeteria for their lunch hour.

Big Joe was a gigantic inflatable cactus that soared over the tables in the back corner of the cafeteria. He'd been put up for Back to the Alamo Day during spirit week the previous year. Wearing red sunglasses and a ridiculous cowboy hat on top of its head, which skimmed the ceiling of the cafeteria, Big Joe was instantly adopted by the student body. The students refused to take their lunchtime mascot down, even after spirit week was long over.

"Let's just say, he's gone volleyball crazy!"

As soon as they entered the cafeteria, Neeka stopped in her tracks. Today, Big Joe had a special costume on. Taped to his sunglasses were two volleyballs, one on each lens, the right one spelling out *JV* and the left one *Varsity* in blue glitter lettering. In his arms, he held a banner that read: "The girls of the v-ball team will make you scream! Go volleyball!"

The effect was quite theatrical, particularly since poor Joe needed a good inflating. He looked as if he was melting into loose plastic. With the air conditioning on, his limp cactus arms clapped together, banner in hand.

He's clapping for us, Neeka thought.

It was a far cry from the previous year when half the student body didn't even know there was a volleyball team. Realizing she had been a part of making this happen, where her fellow classmates were just as excited as the team for the first volleyball match of the season, she felt an immense pride. Instantly, she took out her phone to snap a picture to print and hang in her locker.

"Looks like someone better air-up Big Joe quick, or he's gonna tucker out all over the football team," Lacey said, coming up behind them and pointing toward the quarterback and his linesmen eating lunch directly under the cactus. "Great, isn't it?" she added, beaming.

"Sure is," Neeka said, nodding along with Payton.

"Care to join me for lunch?" Lacey asked, looking at Payton specifically. "I'd like to discuss JV, if that's okay?"

"Sounds great," Payton said. "I'll just grab some grub and meet you guys in a few minutes. Where are you sitting?"

Neeka lifted up her lunch bag. "I was thinking we'd eat outside in the shade under the willow?"

Payton nodded and left them for the lunch line.

Lacey inhaled and smiled. "Is that fried shrimp you have there?"

"Left over from my papa's BBQ last night."

"Then lead the way," Lacey said. "Just don't blame me if a few of those shrimp suddenly jump from the bag into my mouth."

Ten minutes later, the three girls sat under the willow tree. The end-of-summer heat would be unbearable if not for the shelter the willow provided with its long, wilting branches. It was quite peaceful, except for the sound of tennis balls slamming across the court nearby. Neeka adjusted her blazer underneath her. She hoped it would keep the summer bugs from crawling up her legs.

Next to her, Lacey grabbed another one of her shrimp. She had eaten nearly half since Neeka had opened her lunch bag. Her cheeks puffed out as she crammed the whole thing into her mouth.

Neeka watched her, amused. "Go right ahead, eat all my shrimp. You'll need all the energy you can get if you want to beat me to the starting line-up," she challenged light-heartedly.

"Girl," Lacey stated, "I don't need your fried shrimp to do that. Last year was the last time I let a freshie set in my place."

Neeka stole a piece of shrimp out of Lacey's hand and ate it herself. "I'm a sophomore this year, remember?"

"Same difference. You're a youngster. I'm a senior. And this year, I'm your worst nightmare." She winked playfully at Payton, who watched silently as the two girls bantered.

"You're only competition 'cos I keep pushing you," Neeka countered. "Better step your game up."

Instead of coming up with another witty remark, Lacey instead tackled Neeka to the dirt, hugging her like a large pet. "I love you, Renika Leigh. And you too, Payton Moore. I'll miss you two when I leave for college next year."

Payton laughed as Neeka tried to wrestle out of Lacey's grip. "I wish Coach Gina allowed us to play on our natural competitiveness more, like you two are doing now. When it's friendly like this, it challenges us to be better, to push ourselves. But Coach Gina is so worried about us all turning into little Annettes, all she does is cheer us on, even when we're acting up. This is volleyball, not a nursery. We're warriors. We need to be treated like the fighters we are. Like in that movie about the girl who has to fight in those games to survive. It's survival."

Letting Neeka go, Lacey sat back against the tree. "We need arrows, not flowers."

"Exactamundo. Can you be our coach, Lacey?" Payton asked, only half joking.

"Cheer up! Coach Gina is an awesome volleyball player. Y'all are lucky to be working with her. I heard a rumor the Vikings want to hire her on after their head coach retires this year."

"As long as it's not Demonbreun High," Neeka protested, scowling as she spoke of their rivals. The Demonbreun High girls were great volleyball players, the best in the district until Hickory Academy's surprise season last year, but what they had in skill, they lacked in sportsmanship.

Their conversation made Neeka think of something else. "Hey, Lacey, do you know what Coach Gina's name was before she was married?"

"My guess?" Lacey asked.

"Yeah?"

"Gina."

Neeka rolled her eyes. "You know what I mean."

"I don't know. Why do you ask?"

"No reason," Neeka mumbled.

"Since we're on the topic, I know the season has only started, but how do you think JV is doing so far?" Lacey asked, rounding back to the reason she had asked to eat lunch with them. "I want to live up to the promise we made to Coach Mike to lead the team this year."

"We're okay, but we're sloppy at times, especially when we're goofing off. It's not like last year. JV isn't as focused as it used to be. The girls are treating it more like a social hour than an opportunity to work on our skills as a team."

"But isn't that right on track with Team Scary Pancake's plan?" Lacey asked. Neeka had told her about the plan one afternoon during varsity practice. "I mean, you gals set out this year to make sure the team was united from the get-go."

"Yeah, but we still need to improve our skills and grow as players. On Tuesday, Courtney and Val were ten minutes late for practice because they took their sweet time chatting on the walk over from the high school to the middle school."

"What did Coach Gina do?" Neeka asked, suddenly curious. If it had been Coach Mike, the girls would have been doing ten minutes of push-ups. Or something equally embarrassing and difficult.

"That's the problem!" Payton exclaimed, becoming emotional. "The girls weren't even told off. Coach Gina just told them she was glad they made it to practice. It was almost as if she was thanking them for showing up!"

"Well, there isn't a lot of competition to be on the JV team. If the girls start to drop out, there won't be enough of you to play," Lacey reckoned.

"That's not a long-term solution," Payton argued. "Coach Gina needs to push us to improve, the way Coach Mike does. Did you know she actually threw in the idea that we might all vote who should be captain of JV? I'd prefer she hold it over our heads and make us fight for it."

"Since you're not practicing with varsity this year, I just assumed you would be captain," Neeka said, frowning. "I thought that was half the reason they decided it was best you practice with JV. So you could take on that role."

"Not if Valerie Sutton has her way. She's delighted at the idea of a vote. But the role of captain isn't supposed to be a popularity contest.

It's supposed to be about the ability to lead well. To motivate."

"I agree," Lacey said. "Volleyball is a fast game that requires a lot of communication. You need a well-appointed leader. If everyone is split up, looking in different directions, then there's no longer a team. No one gets heard."

Neeka remained quiet as the girls continued to talk, unsure if she should speak up on Coach Gina's behalf. She knew what Payton said was correct. The girls needed a healthy amount of competitiveness to drive forward. But if *Diary of a Young Volleyball Star* was the work of Coach Gina, as she suspected, then she knew the woman wasn't being totally irresponsible in her coaching tactics.

According to the book, Coach Gina had a rough time with a very negative coach while she was playing for her college team. It had cut down on her self-esteem. With plans even then to coach in the future, she had vowed in her diary she'd never be so harsh with her own players.

I know the feeling, Neeka thought, reminding herself of the promise she'd made not to lead like Annette had.

****

While the rest of the JV team hollered and jeered around them, Neeka and Payton stood nose to nose, glaring at one another. Frozen in place, they resembled Greek statues as they stared each other down, neither willing to back off. Against her will, Neeka felt her body beg to move, but she wouldn't let Payton win.

It was bestie against bestie.

Their eyes began to water. Neeka couldn't stop from twitching. She fought it as long as possible, but it was useless. Despite her teammates yelling her name beside her, encouraging her on, she broke down.

Falling to the ground, she felt loud bursts of laughter escaping her throat. Even as some of her teammates scowled and groaned at her failure, she couldn't hide her giddiness.

Payton shot her arm up triumphantly.

I'm going to pee my pants if I don't stop laughing, Neeka thought, horrified.

"OMG Payton," she said, gasping for breath. Her ribs were starting to hurt. "You looked like a cross between a puppy dog and a blowfish with your big ole bug eyes. I'm never entering another staring contest with you again. It's impossible to win. I swear you make that fish face on purpose."

Coach Gina stepped forward. "Fair is fair, ladies. Payton, you get to pick what side of the court your team starts the scrimmage on."

"We'll take the strong side," Payton decided, referring to the left-hand side of the court. It was the easier side for right-hand players to attack from.

"Of course you do," Neeka grumbled, though she was still laughing.

Coach Gina pointed to the opposite side of the net. "Weak side, Neeka."

Half of the JV girls trailed behind her, still annoyed that she had lost the staring contest to Payton. Among them was Courtney. Neeka wasn't too familiar with the other girls who had been placed on her scrimmage team, so she was glad Courtney was there. They had spoken a few times in the halls. Courtney seemed cool. Neeka decided to use the scrimmage as an opportunity to get to know her better.

It was the end of the first week of school. Between their summer practices before the school year and the one they'd had on Tuesday, Coach Gina decided it was time for JV to have a friendly scrimmage—teammate versus teammate. She needed Neeka to even out the teams, so she'd pulled her from varsity practice. Even so, they were still a player down on each side.

"I thought you were on varsity," Courtney noted, running up beside her. "What brings you all the way down to the middle school gym?"

"You guys do, of course," Neeka said. "I play for JV too. Just like Payton and Selina."

"But you practice with varsity?" Courtney raised a doubtful eyebrow.

"Well... yeah... I have to. I'm on the varsity starting line-up."

"Unlike Payton and Selina who are only substitutes," Courtney said, understanding.

The comment made Neeka uncomfortable. She hated the way things had turned out, especially for Payton. "Coach Gina asked me to come in today to even out the teams for the scrimmage. I was more than happy to. Like I said, you guys are my team too. Plus, it's an important practice. This will be the first time some of the other JV girls play an actual volleyball match."

Courtney looked down. "Don't remind me. I still don't understand why I wasn't put on varsity. I'm a great hitter, and I've played before."

"Yeah, but varsity has a few seniors that are already hitters. I know it doesn't seem fair, but this is only the start. You have three more years to prove yourself to Coach Mike."

As Neeka took her position as setter, Courtney stood near her, ready to hit.

"Coach Gina too," Courtney mumbled. "I think it's already been decided that Payton and Selina will start as outside hitters. That means I'm bumped to the bench."

Neeka hadn't considered this before. She instantly felt sorry for Courtney. It would be difficult news to swallow, knowing you were a good player yet still had to wait on the bench as a substitute.

"If it makes you feel any better, Janette is in the exact same situation," she informed her. "She transferred here from Memphis last year and replaced Lacey as the substitute setter when she injured her hand right before the District Tournament Final. That means, technically, for one day, Janette was on varsity. But she's still stuck substituting on JV this year because Lacey and I already have varsity under control..."

"And you're also starting for JV," Courtney finished.

"Yeah."

"What, the coaches have a thing against the new girls or something?"

"Sometimes, these things are just a matter of timing." It was all Neeka knew to say.

Across the net, behind Payton and Selina, Val took her position as *libero*. Her game face was on. *Whoa girl.* Instinctively, Neeka felt her muscles tighten, ready for action. Val looked like a bulldozer about to start a rampage.

As *libero*, even though Val could replace any player in the back row of her team, with the JV split in two, there was no one to replace. All the girls were on the court. But it was a useful strategy during an official match.

Hope our own mock libero can keep up, Neeka thought, quickly glancing back to a sophomore on their side. Since neither of the *liberos* were replacing anyone, their roles were purely defense. Coach Gina had altered the rules slightly in favor of the scrimmage, trying to give the girls a real sense of what a match would be like.

"Get ready to dig that ball!" Neeka called out to the sophomore. "Dive for it if you have to. Just don't let it hit the ground. I'll be ready to receive it for the set." As setter, she was usually the second person to touch the ball. She then set it up for the hitters to attack with.

The girl looked uneasy. "I'm a blocker! I'm only playing *libero* because we had to split up for the scrimmage."

"If you can't reach it, then yell help. One of the other girls will pass it to me."

"Help!" she cried.

"Funny," Neeka said without a smile. "Get ready. They're about to serve."

Neeka settled into her own position just as Coach Gina blew the whistle. The ball flew awkwardly toward them, just barely missing the net. The mock *libero* got to it easily enough and passed it on to her. Pushing the ball into the air, she yelled, "Courtney!"

Like a rocket, Courtney slammed the ball over the net; it hit the floor on the other side, too quick for anyone to touch it. A kill shot.

"Amazing work, Courtney!" Coach Gina yelled from the sidelines.

Neeka was impressed. Perhaps Coach Mike had made a mistake leaving Courtney on JV. But as the scrimmage continued, Neeka noticed Courtney's weakness. When she was able to position herself correctly, her shot was solid. But for the most part, her timing was off, causing her to sometimes pass the ball over the net instead of striking it. And when she didn't have time to pass, she dinked it over with her fingertips.

Still, Courtney showed a lot of promise. Not only was she a fantastic hitter, when her timing was right, but she was also a pretty good blocker as well.

"Remember, don't overthink it," Neeka recommended. "Position your body square with the ball and let it flow naturally."

Courtney nodded, acknowledging her advice.

With a little work, that girl will be a fireball, Neeka mused.

Immediately, her thoughts turned to Payton and Selina. Her friends were already up against tough competition on the varsity team. It looked as if Courtney might prove to be a further obstacle in their efforts to make the varsity starting line-up.

By the third and final set, her team was up by one point. It was Neeka's turn to serve. She didn't have a jump shot, not like Payton, but she was decent enough. She hit the ball with force, bending her fingers down slightly, hoping the ball would fall short just beyond the net.

"Mine!" she heard Selina yell. "In your face, Leigh!" she challenged before slamming the ball at Neeka's feet.

Feeling her competitiveness kick in, Neeka hollered toward the girls on her side, "Don't listen to her garble, ladies. Selina's all talk and no action."

"The point I just scored seem pretty action-y to me," Selina retorted.

"Loser buys ice cream," Neeka yelled back.

"With sprinkles!" Payton shouted, getting in on the action.

"Sprinkle this!" County roared as the serve came their way. Neeka set to her, assisting her in a point.

But the other team soon won the serve back. Quickly, Neeka's side surrendered their lead. Growing tired, her girls were losing focus and kept fumbling around the court. With Selina already celebrating her free ice cream on the other side, it took all Neeka's strength not to unleash her inner Annette. When the ball was passed out of bounds or the girls let their arms bend instead of keeping them straight, she bit her lip instead of snapping at the girls to get it together.

Stop messing around! she screamed inwardly. Then she reprimanded herself. *Calm down. You're meant to a better leader than Annette ever was. That means having patience. A lot of these girls are new to things like setting and spiking. They'll get there.*

To prove to herself she would not turn into Annette, she spent the rest of the match helping the girls as much as she could. Instead of making a huge display of a player's weaknesses, like Annette had done, Neeka would quietly go up to a teammate and give her a few tips in between points. If someone was out of position, she'd dive for the ball herself.

In the end, they lost. A lot of that was thanks to Val. She was a feisty *libero*, not yet ready for varsity, but she would grow. Fear was definitely not an issue. The girl looked like a gymnast, falling to the floor and rolling out of dives. The main issue Neeka noticed was her passing. If she conquered that, she'd be a hot contender on the court.

Payton and Selina were also a great pair when they worked together. Payton still had a lot of work to do on her spike. It lacked the authority Courtney and Selina had. But her timing was excellent. And she had tuned into when it was better to tip the ball over instead of spiking it, making it difficult for Neeka's team to block.

But Neeka did notice one thing she was definitely not happy about. She thought she was imagining it at first, but by the end of the match, it was becoming more and more obvious. Whenever Payton made a mistake, Val would whisper to one of the other girls, and they both would snicker. She didn't know what was happening, but it was odd. She'd played with Val in basketball. Though the girl was determined, Neeka never knew her to be nasty.

"Let's get a team photo so I can post it on Twitter," Val said after they all shook hands. "Our very first scrimmage!"

As they lined up, Neeka kept a close eye on Val.

It seemed Hickory Academy's newest sweetheart wasn't so sweet after all.

****

"So where are we headed?" Selina asked, bounding up to Neeka at the end of practice.

At that moment, a bright orange jeep came into the parking lot, blasting a polka CD at full blast. Around her, the other volleyball girls and athletes waiting for their lifts home started to giggle at the upbeat folk music.

"The only place I'm headed this evening is to prison, after I kill my brother."

"You'd look awful in stripes," Val remarked, joining them.

Jamari pulled up in front of her and stuck his head out of the window while the music continued to blare. "Hi sis! I'm playing your favorite MP3."

"It's not mine, and it's not an MP3. It's Papa's CD," Neeka corrected him, but the awful noise drowned her out.

Jamari turned the music off then loudly repeated for everyone around to hear, "I said, Neeka Leigh, that I was playing your favorite MP3. You know, that polka band you love sooo much, you've downloaded all their music."

"I'm sorry, Jamari Leigh," Neeka bellowed, equally as loud. "But I had to start listening to that awful polka music to drown out how you cry yourself to sleep every night because you're afraid of the dark."

"I don't do that!" Jamari protested. Still leaning out the window, he turned his head toward the crowd. "Honestly, I don't do that!"

"So... what about that ice cream?" Selina asked. "Where are we going?"

"I've got to get home," Neeka said reluctantly. "But how about tomorrow afternoon? I'm sure I can convince crybaby here to give us a lift somewhere."

Jamari ignored her.

"I don't care when you pay up, as long as you pay up," Selina

31

boasted cheerfully, the spirit of the weekend on her. "Nice ride," she said to Jamari. "I preferred it when it was silver, but the orange doesn't look too bad. Laters."

As Neeka was about to jump into the jeep, Val said, "So, Neeka, *this* is your brother." She smiled at Jamari. "I saw you a few times at our middle school basketball games, but that was ages ago. We were never introduced."

Neeka mentally rolled her eyes. Was Val for real? She was hitting on Jamari? She must have cotton buds between her ears, because no girl in their right mind would want Jamari for a boyfriend.

She almost said as much, but decided it was best not to insult her teammate. The girl would have to figure it out on her own. "Yes, *this* is my brother, Jamari," Neeka said.

Jamari was barely listening. "I hate to stop the party, ladies, but I've got a hot date tonight."

Val's face fell.

"Don't be fooled. He means with a big screen TV and a game controller," Neeka informed her. "He's been addicted to Battle for Earth, or whatever it's called, for ages."

Val laughed. "I love video games."

You've probably never played one in your life, Neeka guessed.

She elbowed her brother in the ribs. "Jamari, this is Valerie Sutton. She's on the JV team with me."

"Soon to be varsity," Val added.

"Yeah, cool. I'm Jamari."

"We established that already," Neeka groaned.

Val pursed her lips together. "Well, Jamari, it was a pleasure to meet you." She then smiled coyly and walked away.

"Time to save planet Earth!" Jamari announced, starting the jeep.

"You're an idiot," was all Neeka had the energy to say.

CHAPTER 4

The trouble with being on an athletic scholarship in college is that volleyball doesn't feel the same. Before, it was a passion of mine. Now, it feels like a job. I still enjoy it, immensely, but I'm starting to favor the meetings down at the community center more than my practices at the university. Though my family can afford to pay my college tuition, my grades weren't spectacular in high school. I know the only reason this college accepted my application was because of my volleyball skills. It's a great school. I want to be here, so I won't let anyone down. But part of me can't help but feel that I would prefer to be here without the athletic scholarship.

I'm still one of the best players on the court, but it is strange moving up from a high school team onto a college team. In high school, teams are formed purely based on what girls happen to live in the district for each school. Coaches have to work with what they have. But in college, the teams are essentially hand-selected long before the school year starts. All the girls on my college team are good. Really good. In a way, it's refreshing. I love the thrill of working with some of the best college volleyball players in possibly the entire world. But, if I'm truly honest, diary, it's also a bummer. I'm still a star, but not the way I was in high school. When we play a match, I'm not the main focus of the game. I share the limelight now.

Maybe it's a good thing. It means there's not as much pressure on my shoulders. I'm thankful for that, given what a horrible coach we have. He never has anything nice to say. All he does is shout and scream. My guess is that he was either once a hit man for the mob, or he simply has no clue what makes a good coach. I mean really. The other day, Cynthia missed the ball. There was no way she could have reached it! It was like a totally killer shot. We're good, but we're still restricted by the laws of physics. Coach didn't see it that way. After the match, he made a show of her in front of the entire team. She was trying not to cry, but I could see how hard she was taking it. And then, at the end of his rant, when she tried to give an explanation, he told her that the reason she missed the ball was because she was gaining too much weight and needed to lose a few pounds.

I have never wanted to punch someone so hard in my life! Cynthia is so slim! But now, the poor girl is afraid to eat anything. Which is so unhealthy. Because of jerks like Coach, women athletes somehow get this false idea that not eating will help their game. But that's so not true. Not at all! The opposite is true. Going hungry makes an athlete weak, tired, and dizzy. They can't focus. They move slower. Overall, going hungry makes someone a worse player, not a better one. Also, if Coach was in any way good at what he does, he would know that when the body goes into hunger mode, one of the first things it burns off is muscle. Muscle! The one thing all athletes need is muscle. We can't perform otherwise! What a jerk. Telling an athlete she needs to lose a few pounds is about as useless as a screen door on a submarine.

I think tomorrow I'm going to pull Cynthia aside and let her know how unhealthy it is not to eat. How it could destroy her career as a volleyball player. I'll even tell her about the article I read about the girl who almost died because she was so obsessed with losing weight. Then I'll take her out to a huge steak dinner! I'm honestly thinking about reporting Coach to some higher authority. This is not right. I'm so angry!

At least I'm meeting Tyler tonight. It's our second date. He's so gorgeous! I really hope he goes to my volleyball match next week...

****

Zowzers.

Neeka put the book down. It was her study hall period in the library, but she couldn't stop reading *Diary of a Young Volleyball Star*. Now, more than ever, she was absolutely convinced it was written by Coach Gina. It just made sense. Neeka remembered a lecture Coach

Gina had given them last year about being healthy, to make sure they kept good, nutritious food in their diet and always had plenty of fuel in their stomachs before a practice or match. She'd warned them about the dangers of eating disorders. How their hair and teeth could fall out. And how no sport was worth putting the body through such struggle.

"You can't play volleyball if you're passed out on the court," Coach Gina had said.

Neeka looked back at the cover. It had a sky blue background and green lettering with lots of volleyballs and hearts around the title. She didn't need to flip through the pages for a hundredth time to know there were no photos. And from what she had read so far, there were no actual references to any schools. High school was just called high school. College was just college. Perhaps the publisher had done that on purpose. The Coach the author wrote about probably wouldn't have been too happy if, with his awful coaching ethic, he'd been named in a book.

"Just give me some clue," Neeka said softly, picking at a sticker of Justin Timberlake on the back cover.

"Shhhh," said a boy next to her.

"Don't shush me, George. I see those wireless headphones you have stitched into your ears," she hissed back.

He removed the headphones. "Is Payton in love with me yet?" he asked quietly.

"No. She has better taste than that."

"Do you think she'll go to the homecoming dance with me?"

Oh my stars, he was persistent.

"George," she said patiently, "Payton does not dance. Not unless it's at the end zone of a football field. If you were a basketball and she could throw you into a hoop, you might have a shot."

"Thanks!" George said happily, then put his headphones back in, ending the conversation.

Neeka was confused at his reaction but shrugged her shoulders and continued reading the book.

****

"Fantastic job today, girls!" Coach Gina said after blowing her whistle to end practice. "We just need to tighten up some of those passes, but you all deserve a gold star!"

"Some of us more than others," Courtney said under her breath, but Neeka heard.

Just then, a fire drill sounded.

"See, you were too hot to handle!" their coach joked. "Leave your backpacks here. You can collect them after we're allowed back in the building to change."

The first match of the JV season was upon them. They only had a few days to prepare. Once again, Coach Gina had pulled Neeka from varsity to help the girls get battle ready. Many of the new freshmen were nervous, having never played a match before, not at a competitive level. Neeka knew working with JV would be a good time to practice her leadership skills, so she'd agreed, not that she had much choice.

"Last time, Williams!" Coach Mike had warned his assistant coach, but Coach Gina hadn't seemed at all bothered.

"This is so unfair," Valerie complained as the girls filtered outside. "Why do we have to pay attention to some middle school fire drill? I still don't understand why we can't just practice in the small gym at the high school."

"The table tennis club have the small gym," Payton reminded her. "They're scheduled in to practice on the same days we are."

Val wasn't swayed. "Then why can't the school just change the schedule around? I mean, do you know how embarrassing it is walking to the middle school every practice?"

"They ain't gonna change the schedule 'cos the dance team has the small gym the other days of the week," Selina answered as the team lined up outside at the designated assembly point. "I was thinking of joining dance, since it doesn't interfere with volleyball."

"What!?" Payton and Neeka cried in unison.

"I have years of ballet under my belt," Selina insisted.

36

The blank faces on the rest of the girls said it all. It wasn't that dance wasn't a worthy team to be on. It was just a shock hearing it from Selina. The dance girls were some of the most glamorous girls in the school. They had hair extensions and perfect make-up. And though Selina did like a heavily lined eyelid, she was more rock chic than glam girl.

Suddenly, Selina burst out laughing. "Man, the look on your faces. Priceless! Of course I'm not joining dance. Who do you think I am, Ashley Tisdale?"

Valerie stood up straighter. "Good. You need to focus on your v-ball skills if you want to make the varsity starting line-up next year."

Selina shot her a look that screamed, *Who do you think you are telling me that, frosh!?* But Neeka set a hand on her shoulder, indicating for her to let it go.

A few minutes later, they were allowed back into the school. The team immediately headed toward the girls' locker room to change, except for Selina, who returned to the gym.

"She's hardly still mad about Valerie's comment?" Payton asked Neeka as they pulled their normal clothes out of their lockers. It was too hot to put their uniforms back on, so many of the girls brought their street clothes to change into after practice. It meant they had to carry around three sets of clothes on practice days, but it was worth it, especially on a scorcher.

"I don't think so," Neeka said. "She's probably just getting something from her backpack." She hesitated, then added, "You know, George was asking about you today in study hall."

Payton blushed. "Was he? That's sweet."

"Do you think you'll ever give him a chance?"

Payton shook her head. "I like him, as a friend. But I don't 'like him' like him. Plus, I'm not allowed to date anyone until I'm sixteen. For once, both of my parents were in agreement about that. Actually, my dad said I should wait until I was thirty-five, but my mom laughed it off."

"Does that mean your parents are talking again?" Neeka hoped so, for Payton's sake. Though Payton rarely shared her emotions out loud, at least regarding serious things like this, she saw how stressful it had been for her friend to have parents who gave each other the silent treatment, except for when it came to arranging visits and other parental concerns.

"Yeah. They are. Kind of. When my dad comes to pick me up on weekends when I go to Cincinnati to visit him, my mom no longer treats him like he's some sort of escaped convict. They actually make small talk."

"Well, it's a start."

"It is. By the time I graduate in a few years, they might actually have a full conversation," she said, smiling with good humor.

The last to leave the locker room, by the time Neeka and Payton returned to the gym, most of the girls had either left or were waiting around indoors, under the cool blasts from the air conditioner, for their rides to show up.

"I can't wait for it to snow," Courtney said, leaning back on a bleacher while she splashed cool water on her face from her water bottle. "It does snow here, right?"

"Yep," Neeka said. "Well, sometimes. I thought you were from California. Aren't you used to the heat?"

"San Francisco," Courtney specified. "The north of California is a lot colder than the south."

"I mistook you for an LA beach babe," Val said. "You could easily pass as a famous model. Come here, I want to show you something."

Neeka watched as Val lead Courtney toward her equipment bag, where a few other girls were waiting. She pulled out a knee pad, signed by some local sports star. The girls then bent their heads low, no doubt gossiping about something. Soon, they broke into laughter.

Payton approached the group, obviously trying to fit in with the other JV girls. But as soon as she poked her head over the crowd to see what was happening, the girls instantly went quiet, as if the conversation was over.

"Cool autograph!" she said enthusiastically before leaving the girls to re-join Neeka on the bleachers. She tried to wipe away the look of distress on her face, but it wouldn't budge.

"Why do they always do that?" she said to Neeka.

"Do what?" Neeka asked, though she had witnessed the whole thing.

She didn't want to hurt Payton's feelings further by telling her what she suspected—that Val was slowly trying to push Payton out. Neeka wasn't exactly sure what was happening. Her instincts as Payton's friend were to stand up for her, but she had to take her responsibilities as a leader into account as well. Once she understood the situation more, she would do something to fix it.

"They never tell me what they're talking about," Payton clarified, discouraged.

Neeka waved her hand. "Who cares? It's just silly frosh talk. They're probably all excited about the new Barbie doll being released. We're sophomores. We have more important things to think about."

Payton seemed satisfied by this. "Okay. Sure. Hey, what's Selina doing?"

Still dressed in her practice clothes, Selina emerged from the equipment room, pulling with her a stand filled with balls. She had her usual look of determination on her face as she hauled the stand over toward the net.

"Hey, Leigh, will you shag for me?" she shouted.

Neeka sighed inwardly. She was tired after school and practice. The last thing she wanted to do was chase after balls as Selina hit them. But she knew it was her duty as a friend to help. "What for?" she hollered back.

A flash of regret crossed Selina's face, but she quickly replaced it with a firm resolve. "You'll see."

"Fine," Neeka gave in. "But Jamari is already on his way to pick me up. I can't stay long."

Along with the rest of the JV girls still around, she watched as Selina grabbed a ball and stood behind the end line to serve. Throwing the ball high in the air, she took a few steps forward, jumped up, and pounded the ball. It went straight into the net.

Next to her, Payton gasped.

Selina was practicing a topspin jump serve—Payton's signature

39

move. As it stood, Payton was the only girl in the district who could successful perform the jump serve. It was her anchor to varsity, the only reason she was a substitute. Coach Mike called her in whenever he wanted to cream the competition.

But Neeka didn't think Payton had anything to worry about. Payton's height gave her a clear advantage. Not only could Payton deliver the serve, but she did it well, especially after a year of further practice. Her serves were nearly unstoppable. Selina was just starting out. It'd be awhile before she caught up to Payton.

As Neeka thought about it further, she came to the conclusion that having two girls who could do a topspin jump serve would probably be a huge asset to their team, especially next year when there was a chance Payton and Selina would start for varsity. If she had it her way, all the girls would know how to do the serve. Then they'd be one of the best teams in the nation!

Selina continued to practice. Neeka, as promised, collected the balls for her. It was easy enough to do. Most of the balls landed in the net. Selina mistakenly assumed that, because the serve was hard to do, it required extra force. The truth was, aim and precision had more to do with the serve than force. The point of the jump serve was to land the ball in any area of the court across the net the server chose. If the ball didn't go where it was meant to, it was ineffective. When she didn't hit the ball as hard, her aim was better, and she usually got it over the net.

"Neeka, your phone is ringing!" Payton shouted from the bleachers.

Neeka tossed the ball in her hand into the hammock-style stand. "That's my brother. Gotta go. Nice work, Selina."

Selina gave her a thumbs up before returning to the serve.

Payton followed Neeka out into the parking lot, her backpack and equipment bag in hand.

"You need a lift home?" Neeka asked. "According to his text, Jamari will be here in about five minutes."

"I was actually wondering if you wanted to head to that smoothie joint down the road?" She seemed agitated.

"Now?" Neeka asked. "But Jamari is nearly here."

"Can you just call him and ask if he can pick you up in an hour or so? It's really important. Tell him you'll meet him at the smoothie place."

It wasn't like Payton to be so forward. Something was definitely up. Neeka had two choices—annoy her brother or upset Payton. She never minded annoying her brother, so Payton won.

"Okay," she agreed. "But I'll have to promise Jamari a smoothie. The Jalapeno Death Bed should do just fine."

****

On such a hot evening, the line into the smoothie place was incredibly long. It snaked out the door and wrapped down the block. As they walked past the entrance, a huge chalkboard sign outside read: "To Go Only." Spotting a few people from their school, they followed the line to the back.

"I hope we get inside before Jamari arrives," Neeka noted.

Payton was hardly listening. "We need to talk," she said.

"Clearly."

"Did you know Selina was working on a jump serve?" Payton asked, her voice rising.

Neeka didn't like the accusation in Payton's voice. Her defenses immediately shot up. What did Payton expect? That no one would ever try to follow her in her footsteps? She couldn't be the only person with a topspin jump serve forever. Selina had every right to practice one.

"No, but why does it matter?"

Payton was outraged. "How can you even ask that?"

"Listen, I know why you're upset. You and Selina are friends, but you're also competing for varsity. But didn't last year teach you anything, Payton? You can't excel at everything. Just do your best and see what happens. Anyway, you're excellent at the serve. Why are you so threatened?"

41

"Because Coach Mike already favors Selina over me as it is."

"Well, you should take it as a compliment that she's working on a jump serve. Imitation is the highest form of flattery, as my ma always says."

"This isn't Selina trying to imitate me. She's stealing my move," Payton whined.

Neeka felt her inner Annette start to rise. "You don't own the jump serve," she snapped.

Payton put her hands on her hips. "Why are you being so harsh? Didn't *you* learn anything from last year, Neeka? Our friendship is more important than volleyball. It's more important than any sport. Don't go back to choosing your newfound fame over me."

Neeka swallowed her words like they were a sour apple. Just because they were friends didn't mean Neeka had to agree with Payton about everything. Not that Payton asked her too. She was usually pretty quiet about these things, but Selina practicing a jump serve had switched her trigger. Still, she was being childish. Friends with Selina as well, Neeka really didn't want to hear about any issues they had with each other.

"Listen, let's change the subject," she said, suddenly wishing Jamari hadn't agreed to pick her up later. "So just a heads up, George is likely going to ask you to the homecoming dance…"

As they talked, Neeka had the stark realization that being a team leader sometimes meant abandoning her responsibilities as a friend. When it really came down to it, should the need ever arise, she wasn't sure she would be willing to put the team before Payton. They'd known each other since elementary school. Payton was like a sister to her. And family always came first.

42

CHAPTER 5

Payton felt totally lost.

Around her, her fellow JV teammates scrambled for the ball. Time after time, they collided into each other in their haste. There was no strategy to their game. It was pandemonium, like little kids running around at recess.

And worse, no one seemed to care. No one except Team Scary Pancake. The other JV girls were actually laughing, as if the whole spectacle was a joke.

I wish it were a joke, Payton thought.

She had no idea what to do, unsure of how far her role as a team leader reached. Did she yell at them to get their act together? Or was that too Annette-like? Their performance had nothing to do with lack of skill. They simply weren't committed to the game, talking between serves and pointing out cute guys in the bleachers. Someone needed to say something to them, quickly.

At the sideline, Coach Gina did very little. She applauded them when they made a good move, and she gave pointers that would be helpful, if the girls were listening, but she refused to reprimand them on their bad attitude. Even monkeys could pass a ball now and again. The JV girls need guidance, in the form of a good telling off, but Coach Gina wasn't offering it.

"Concentrate on the ball. Get in your ready positions before each serve," was the only constructive feedback Payton heard her make.

"We can't afford to lose any more points due to violations," Neeka shouted to the team, taking charge. "Remember, you can't move from your rotation until *after* the ball is in play."

Across their side of the court, Neeka looked at Payton with concern while Selina looked at the scoreboard, shaking her head.

This was worse than last year. The JV team had never been champions, but they'd always played a lot better than this. Granted, it was only their second match of the season, and both had been away games. Payton knew it was too early to start comparing them to previous years', but she couldn't help it. A team's biggest competition was past teams from their school. That's how a team improved, moved forward to become champions.

The ball flew toward them, heading straight for a sophomore in the back corner. "Got it," she chirped and lunged feebly forward, but her angle was off. Instead of sending the ball to Neeka to set, it flew out of bounds, all the way into the bleachers.

"Oops," she said giddily.

Oops? What was this, Pin the Tail on the Donkey? "Oops" didn't cut it. This was volleyball, not some party game.

Their one saving grace was Val. If it weren't for their *libero*, they'd probably already be on the bus home, defeated. But Val was growing tired. Payton could see it in her face. The other team was way more experienced, and there was only so much Val could do on her own without the help of her fellow teammates.

Serves you right, Payton thought, momentarily forgetting they were on the same team.

Val was partially to blame for this. Usually the one to distract the girls with rumors and chitchat while Coach Gina tried to give them instruction during practice, Val was the ringleader of the JV team's bad attitude. She had encouraged the girls to stop taking practice seriously. And now they were all paying the price.

When Val missed a few digs in a row, Neeka started running for the ball herself, prepping it for the hitters, but Hickory Academy's offense was as disorganized as their defense. Payton was finding it hard to control her spikes, making it easy for the other team to block her. Unfortunately, she couldn't put it down to attitude. She had been paying attention during practice.

However, her game wasn't totally off. Her jump serve was strong, as usual. When she served, the other side had a hard time returning it. But she sometimes got in her own way, losing concentration and sending the ball into the net. When it happened, she would sense the hope in her team deflating.

You can't spend the whole match goofing off then show disappointment because I made a small error, she wanted to tell them.

They were playing the best out of five. In their third set and well behind the other team, Payton would consider it a miracle if the match went on any further.

Maybe it was a good thing their first two JV matches had been away games. It gave them time to work out their kinks. After the disaster today was proving to be, Payton wished on her hands and toes that they were able to get it together for their first home match a few days away. She knew it would draw in a lot of students, mostly because of the varsity match afterwards. They should want to be at their best for it, but JV was in no shape to do the school proud.

It'd be a different story if they were trying their best. But from what Payton could see, they were doing their best at not trying.

Before they had a chance to miss another shot, Coach Gina called a time-out. It was a relief. Maybe she was finally going to rearrange their attitude.

"How are y'all doing?" the woman asked as they huddled together.

"Uh... terrible," Selina answered bluntly.

"Don't get too discouraged, honey. We all just need a little practice, is all."

"Speak for yourself," Selina grumbled.

Coach Gina ignored her.

"I'm about to collapse," one of the sophomores moaned. "Can you sub someone in for me?"

Coach Gina looked at her with sympathy. "Of course. Courtney, you're going to play middle-blocker."

"Finally!" Courtney was tickled. She'd been fix'n to get in.

"Remember, girls. I want you all to have fun out there," Coach Gina said pointedly.

But winning is fun, Payton thought.

As if hearing her thoughts, her coach turned to her. "Payton, I don't want you to worry so much about attacking the ball. Right now, we need your jump serve. Save your energy for that."

She informed the ref of the substitution then said, "Smile girls. Happy thoughts," before sending them back out onto the court.

Smile? That was it? Payton could think of much better speeches to motivate a losing team. *Come on, girls. Play like your life depends on it. If you don't pay attention, you'll never be able to anticipate what the other team is doing.*

"Smile," Selina mocked under her breath as they took their positions.

Putting Courtney in did prove helpful. Full of energy, she turned out to be a talented blocker, helping Hickory Academy recover a few points. As their score increased, so did their focus. Selina reclaimed her title as the best hitter on the JV team, and Val dove hard for the ball. It was enough to take them to a fourth set, but they lost there, ending the match.

"I'm so proud of you girls!" Coach Gina cheered as they came in after the handshake. "Well done today. I saw some major improvement from our last match. Just keep at it and you'll get there." After another round of compliments, she walked away to talk to a few parents calling for her attention.

Selina wiped away the sweat on her forehead with her jersey. "Is she blind? We did horribly today," she criticized, her voice muffled under the jersey.

"I'm calling an emergency meeting of Team Scary Pancake," Neeka declared. "We have about an hour to kill before Coach Mike and the other varsity girls arrive for our other match tonight."

They quickly changed into their varsity jerseys then found a spot under the stairs in the hallway. The needed somewhere private to talk where the JV girls wouldn't overhear. Payton sat on a folded blue mat with Neeka while Selina took a seat on the ground, stretching her legs.

"These double match days are hard," Selina groaned. "We haven't even played tonight's match and my knee is already sore."

"You should start wearing a magnetic knee pad," Payton said wholeheartedly. "I do. It helps the blood flow."

Selina nodded but didn't say anything.

"So what are we going to do about JV?" Neeka asked. "I've only practiced with you guys twice, but even I can see a serious disconnect on the team."

"Our chemistry is all off," Payton stated. "We have a weird energy. It's like being on a massive sugar buzz. On the outside, everything seems okay, but inside, something feels wrong in the gut. Off center. Like being dizzy and not knowing why." Payton picked at the mat, her concern growing.

"After that match, I feel more aggravated than dizzy. This needs to stop."

"I'm not sure how to fix it. Varsity took all the experienced players. Most of the girls on JV have never played before, even some of the sophomores."

"That's no excuse," Selina quipped, joining in. "Just because they haven't played volleyball doesn't mean they haven't played other sports. They know playing a sport requires a certain amount of sacrifice and concentration. Maybe we should talk to Coach Gina."

"No," Neeka protested urgently.

Payton felt her friend tense next to her. She hoped Neeka was all right.

"I mean, it might just cause further problems. Coach Gina might take it as a personal reflection on her," Neeka rationalized.

"It is!" Selina said.

"Or," Neeka continued, "the other JV girls might think we're being sneaky. This is high school. We're expected to work out our own issues. That's why Coach Mike made us team leaders. It's the whole reason Team Scary Pancake even exists."

Wow, Neeka was really taking this leadership role seriously. Payton was impressed. And inspired. She'd been friendly with the other girls, or tried to at least, but she hadn't really led them, not like she did her basketball team. Part of being a leader meant commanding respect. They would never earn the girls' respect if they went to Coach Gina to solve their problems for them.

"Unless it gets really bad, I agree with Neeka," she declared. "Let's take the next few days to think up some strategies to get the girls to take things more seriously. In the meantime, Selina, while we're sitting on the bench at tonight's match waiting to be subbed in, we can try to point out to the JV girls the things varsity are doing right. Perhaps that will inspire them."

****

An excitement that had been absent during the JV match rippled through the crowd as the varsity girls took over the court. Sitting on the edge of her seat next to Selina and the other subs, with the JV girls on the floor, Payton enjoyed the change in energy. Anticipation replaced the stale atmosphere that had descended upon them after JV's loss.

"Hey girls, see how fierce they look," Payton remarked, pointing to her varsity teammates on the court. "They're totally focused. They want this win. They hunger for it. You can see it in their faces."

The JV girls ignored her, immediately jumping into a conversation about homecoming dresses.

Give it time, Payton consoled herself. *They're pretending not to listen, but they hear me.*

Selina didn't seem to mind that the girls on the floor had blocked them out of their conversation, but Payton would be lying if she said it didn't bother her. She couldn't understand what she'd done wrong. She knew she shouldn't care what a group of younger girls thought about her. But she felt lonely. With Neeka practicing with varsity, that only left Selina to talk to. And after learning Selina was working on a jump serve, Payton wasn't too eager to hang out with her. She knew Selina saw it as friendly competition, but Payton felt as though her friend had

48

betrayed her.

As the varsity team took an early lead, Payton tried again with the JV girls. "Look there. See how well they communicated during that play. Their shots are so deadly because they pay attention to the competition and to each other."

"Yes, Coach," Val said, rolling her eyes.

The other girls made an obvious show that they were bored by her comments.

"Don't sound so sassy," Selina warned Val and her group. "If Coach Mike doesn't see some improvement, none of you guys will make it onto varsity next year."

This shut Val up for the rest of the match, but no matter how hard Payton and Selina tried to get through to the JV girls, it was obvious their main focus was less on the game and more on their social lives.

Great, Payton moaned inwardly. *Team Scary Pancake wanted the full cob, but all we got was an empty pot.*

****

During Geometry the next day, an office assistant came into class to hand Payton a note.

Lunch. My office.

It was from Coach Mike.

Any hope of Payton concentrating on hypotenuses went out the window. What did Coach Mike want? Was he going to demote her to JV permanently? Had Coach Gina overheard Team Scary Pancake talking about her under the stairs and now they were off the team?

The air in the room suddenly felt a lot stuffier. She loosened the collar of her polo shirt, wishing she could take off her blazer. Who had decided on blazers in Nashville, of all places? Couldn't they have stuck with cardigans? Or better yet, just gone with T-shirts?

At one point, her Geometry teacher stopped the class to ask if she was all right. "You look as nervous as a long-tailed cat in a room full of rocking chairs," the woman observed.

"I'm fine," Payton said sheepishly.

Lunch eventually arrived. Unable to bring her legs to march toward Coach Mike's office, Payton stalled, dropping her books off at her locker and splashing cool water against her face in the bathroom.

Finally, when she knew she couldn't avoid it anymore, she took small, teetering steps toward the office of doom on the second floor.

"Why ya walking like a penguin?" George asked, catching up to her, clearly happy he'd spotted her in the hallway.

"Sorry, George, I can't talk right now. I have a meeting with Coach Mike."

"Oh, sounds bad. You okay?"

"I don't know yet," she said honestly then left him standing alone.

When she reached the office, she knocked quietly on the door. When Coach Mike didn't answer, she knocked again. She thought she'd gotten lucky and he wasn't in, but then she saw his shadow cross underneath the door. Pressing slightly against the wood, she found the door unlocked, so she pushed it open completely.

Coach Mike was turned away from her, but she could see the giant DJ-like headphones he had on. He spun around and started moonwalking backward, totally lost in his music.

Payton didn't know if she should run or laugh. Frozen in place, she did neither, but only waited for Coach Mike to notice she was there.

When he did, he danced over toward her, keeping his headphones on. He was certainly in a good mood. Beckoning her in with his hand, he pointed toward the whiteboard. In blue marker, he'd written:

HA vs the Cougars – Varsity

Trial Starters – Selina and Payton

Unwilling to surrender his music and dance, he gave her the thumps up. When she returned the gesture, he shooed her out.

In the hallway, Payton did a little dance of her own. She was starting! It was her very first time starting for varsity. Unsure if it would actually happen, she'd been waiting for this day for ages, ever since she'd first been recruited onto varsity last year. Varsity starter—she loved the way it sounded.

Like Hickory Academy, the Brenton Cougars were a new volleyball program. Only in their second year, they would be an easy team to defeat, no matter who started. But Payton didn't let that, or the fact Selina was starting too, ruin her excitement.

"So good news?" George asked, appearing out of nowhere.

"Did you follow me up here?" she asked lightly, too happy to care if he had.

"You looked pretty worried earlier. I wanted to make sure you were okay."

"Thanks!" Payton said with sincerity, then quickly hugged George before skipping away down the hallway to tell Neeka the good news.

****

The big day arrived. Hickory Academy's first home game of the season. Students, teachers, and local fans jammed into the bleachers carrying banners of support that shimmered under the florescent lights of the gymnasium. The loudest among them was Brandon Moore, Payton's father. He'd travelled all the way down from Cincinnati to watch her start. The varsity match wouldn't begin for a little while longer, and already he was sitting up in his seat, trying to get the people around him to do a wave. Jamari joined him.

Next to him, Allison Moore scolded him, fixing her honey blonde pixie cut, embarrassed by all the attention. Lawanda Leigh, Neeka's mother, laughed it off.

Payton quickly waved up at her parents before ducking into the girls' locker room, where she found the rest of the JV team looking glum. They'd lost yet again, but this time, the defeat was bitter. It'd happened on their home turf.

As soon as Val spotted her, she whispered something to the other JV girls, and they all burst into giggles—all except Janette. The Memphis sophomore was distancing herself day by day, seemingly preferring to sit alone than take sides in whatever was happening.

Silently, Payton thanked Janette for it. It was nice to know at least one JV girl hadn't turned against her. Payton wouldn't let their whispers ruin her big day, but it hurt nonetheless.

She didn't have to put up with it for very long. As soon as the other varsity girls entered the locker room to dress, the JV girls went quiet. Varsity was bigger and badder—not a group they wanted to provoke.

"There you are, Payton," Lacey said, giving her a big hug. "Are you excited?"

"Absolutely! More than a tub of banana sauce on a sundae. And you?"

Payton had discovered that Lacey would be starting too. Neeka hadn't minded. After all, as she'd reminded Payton, Lacey had been on the varsity team a lot longer than she had.

"Just like the ole days," Lacey said, winking. "I predict that, between you, Selina, and me, it'll be a solid win."

"I hope you're right," Payton said. She really wanted to prove herself to Coach Mike.

Lacey was. The Cougars had improved since the last time they'd played them, but the team was still developing. Though their JV team had won, their varsity team was no match against Hickory Academy. The home team won with an easy victory.

Selina particularly played a mean game. Payton had no choice but to admit Selina was the better hitter. But for once, Payton didn't mind. Not in this moment. Listening to her dad call her name and the freedom she felt being on a team that completely accepted her, she remembered how much fun volleyball could be. The chemistry on varsity was so different. The girls were really connected, meaning they focused together, fought hard against their competition together, and enjoyed their time on the court together.

She didn't want to go back to JV. She wanted to start practicing with varsity again. Even though she had started for this game, she knew that things would likely go back to normal the following week.

After the mandatory post-match handshake, Neeka grabbed

Payton's arm.

"I'm so glad your dad made it out tonight! Let's go chat with him. I haven't seen Mr. Moore in ages."

Neeka spoke cheerfully, but Payton knew her friend was thinking of her own father. Donald Leigh was a nurse at the hospital. He very rarely made it out to their matches. So far, this was the first match of the season either of their fathers had been at. Payton knew both men would be at every match if they could, but it just wasn't possible, not with Mr. Leigh's late hours and her dad living in Cincinnati.

Together, they bounded up the bleachers to their families. To her disappointment, her mom had slipped out already, but her dad gave her a hug the size of the Deep South.

"Allison decided we should spend some father-daughter time together," he whispered into her ear, explaining her mother's absence. When he let her go, he said more loudly, "All those hours of practice over the year really paid off. That's my champ!"

"Thanks, Dad," Payton said. Her dad was always proud, but as he'd said to her last year, she knew he was most proud of her when it came to volleyball, because unlike most sports, it wasn't something that came naturally to her. She had to work for it. Her success was as much her own will and determination as it was her athleticism.

Val walked by, leaving with her mom. "Hi, Jamari. I'm so glad you came!" she gushed when she saw him.

Caught off guard, Jamari stuttered, "Yeah, um... you're welcome. Well, you know, my sister's here and all."

"I can't wait to see you play during basketball season. I'm a huge fan."

Jamari started bobbing his head up and down awkwardly. "Thanks. That's cool."

Payton glanced at Neeka, speaking with her eyes. *Really?*

She knew Neeka's refusal to look at her was the only way her friend wouldn't spoil the moment by bursting out into uncontrollable laughter.

Val tossed her auburn hair over her shoulder. "See ya again soon."

"Yeah... soon." Jamari lifted his hand in a half-committed wave goodbye.

Payton couldn't hold her amusement in any longer. "Well, at least now she's met the parents," she chuckled.

Neeka bit her tongue, her mind clearly turning.

Not one to miss a beat, after Val was out of earshot, Mrs. Leigh said, "Isn't she on the JV team with you girls?"

"Yeah, she's our *libero*," Neeka answered.

"Well, she doesn't seem very nice. Not to Payton, at least. I was watching her tonight. I'm not impressed," she said sternly.

Yikes! Mrs. Leigh was strict. Payton tried very hard not to get on her wrong side. But she was glad someone cared enough to speak on her behalf.

"It's okay," Payton lied. "She's just jelly."

"She's jam?" her dad asked.

Payton shoved him playfully. "She's jealous. She's always giggling with the other JV girls when I'm around. But I'm taking it as a compliment," she proclaimed with a fake confidence she did not feel regarding the situation. "It's only because they feel threatened by me."

"Well, I won't stand for you being bullied," Mrs. Leigh insisted. "Where is Coach Gina in all this?"

"They don't do it when she's around," Payton clarified.

"Not that Coach Gina would say anything," Neeka added, finally speaking up. "She's all blue skies and sunshine. She doesn't see how much JV is falling apart."

It shocked Payton to hear Neeka say it. Until now, Neeka had always jumped to Coach Gina's defense, telling her she would understand if she read *Diary of a Young Volleyball Star*. This was the first of the old opinionated Neeka Payton had seen in a long time.

"Girls," Mrs. Leigh said, "be real. I could see something was off from all the way up here in the bleachers."

"I don't understand why Gina wouldn't address the younger girls' behavior," Brandon stated.

"Well, I like Gina, but after hearing all this, I question her ability to coach," Mrs. Leigh concluded, surprising everyone.

"I'm not sure that's fair," her dad objected. "Coaches can't always control how their team members are behaving, especially if they're not around to see it. If she was too preoccupied to notice it tonight, then I do believe she should be informed of the situation, but we shouldn't judge her until she knows the full scope of what's happening."

"It's her job to already know," Mrs. Leigh insisted. "As a parent, we can't use the excuse that we didn't know. We have to constantly be observing. What good is a coach if she can't see what's going on right in front of her own nose?"

CHAPTER 6

"Jamari!" Neeka shouted, calling for his attention though she was only standing two feet away from him. "I know you can hear me!"

In front of her, Jamari twisted and turned in his floor-chair, headphones on and controller in hand as he played a videogame.

"I'm in the second quadrant." He spoke into the microphone attached to the headphones. "Enemies are clear."

Maybe he really doesn't hear me, Neeka realized.

God, her brother's room stank. It smelled of stale pizza, which, looking around at the old pizza boxes, was probably exactly what it was. It gave her an idea.

"Pizza time!" she yelled at the top of her lungs.

"Huh?" Jamari turned around. "Pizza?"

"I knew that would get your attention." She smirked. Jamari and pizza. It was an easy formula.

The flat screen in front of them flashed red and showed Jamari's character falling to the ground. He threw the controller on the floor. "Great. Now I have to start from Command Central."

"You're a big boy, you'll survive," Neeka told him.

He looked annoyed. "What do you want, anyway?"

"Can I talk to you?" She took a seat on his messy bed, hoping she didn't crush his lost hamster as she did. The cage looked suspiciously empty.

"You already broke my concentration and got me killed, so I guess," he said, turning off the game console. "What about?"

"Volleyball."

"Don't tell me you and Team Scaredy Pants had a fight."

"Team Scary Pancake, and no, we're fine. But I can't say the same for the rest of the JV team."

Reading how upset she was, he switched to big brother mode. "Yeah, I heard part of the conversation you guys had with Ma and Mr. Moore after the match last night. What exactly is happening?"

"That's the mystery," Neeka said. "I don't understand it. The girls are being rude toward Payton, and I'm not sure why. But more than that, they don't seem at all interested in winning. Why join a team if you don't want to win?"

"I don't know... maybe to make friends, experience new things, travel..."

Neeka held her hands up. "Okay, okay. I get your point. But that's not good enough. The girls on varsity take volleyball very seriously. They don't want to pass their legacy down to a bunch of girls with no passion or respect for the sport. Imagine if the same was true for your basketball team."

"Yeah, gotcha," Jamari said. A student at a magnet school across town, he was captain of his high school basketball team. "Is this the reason JV isn't playing so well? I mean, I hate to say it, but you haven't won a single match yet. It's kinda weird, since your varsity team is undefeated."

"The attitude of the JV girls is a large part of it. How can they play well when they don't even care? And it's not like Coach Gina is doing anything about it. I just don't understand her."

Neeka thought back to the book she was reading. The girl in the pages seemed to have so much tenacity. She stood her ground, fighting on other's behalf. The Coach Gina at present was much more of a pushover. Where had her backbone gone?

"Forget about her for now." Jamari kicked a pile of his clothes aside, looking for something, but Neeka wasn't sure what. Normally, their ma would never stand for such a messy room, but since Jamari was almost eighteen and leaving home next summer, her ma let it go, telling him he had to learn the bliss of a clean room for himself. But with that freedom, he was now required to do his own laundry.

"What do you mean? She's our coach."

"Stop focusing on her and start taking responsibility. Sis, you've got to step up. Kick those girls in the pants."

"You mean verbally?"

"Sure. Why not. You're a sophomore. Most of them are freshmen. You're the authority. You and Team Scaredy Pants."

"Team Scary Pancake."

"It's up to you three to teach the team what's acceptable and what's not. Don't back down. Being a leader isn't always about keeping the peace. Sometimes it's about discipline."

"I can't discipline the team!" Neeka protested, horrified at the idea.

"No, not directly. But make sure they know there are consequences to their actions. Have you talked this through with Payton and that rock girl?"

"Selina. Yes. We've discussed it. We're all tired of JV's behavior. It's growing old real quick."

"Well, then you and Team Scaredy Pants need to come up with a plan."

"Team Scary Pancake. Payton said the same thing, but we haven't come up with anything useful yet. We don't know if the girls are just being lazy and mean, or if something deeper is going on."

"There's only one solution, sis." Giving up the search for whatever he was looking for, Jamari turned his game console back on and offered her a controller, but she declined. "You have to go straight to the source."

****

In between classes the following day, Neeka called a Team Scary

Pancake meeting at Payton's locker. They didn't have long to talk, but she couldn't go through the entire day worrying. Her brother was right. They needed a plan, quick. It was in their hands.

"Right, what should we do?" Selina asked "I'm sick of listening to freshies snicker every time my back is turned."

"I think it's me they're laughing at," Payton acknowledged. "But I don't know why."

"Well, it's about to stop. We're going to put an end to it once and for all," Selina said with resolution.

"Thanks," Payton said.

Neeka was slightly amused Payton felt so threated by Selina, yet she was still willing to confide in her so willingly. She hoped that, through their time together as Team Scary Pancake, Payton would accept that Selina meant her no harm, that she was simply fighting for the same thing Payton wanted by practicing a jump serve—more opportunities to start for varsity.

"One thing is for certain. Coach Gina won't do anything to correct the problem. It's up to us to fix this," Neeka said. "We need to figure out why the new players, particularly the freshmen, aren't willing to put in the work necessary to improve. They're getting a free ride, but that ride is about to end."

"We could spy on them," Selina suggested eagerly. "You know, dress in black and go all CIA on them. Agent Cho at your service."

Neeka laughed. "The spy stuff again? Is that your solution for everything?"

"Yeah," Selina said, as if it were obvious.

"My brother recommended we talk to them directly."

Payton was hesitant. "That might make things worse. They might feel threatened and close us out for good."

"So," Selina said. "At least then they'll know not to mess with us."

"Selina..." Payton persisted. "You're not the one being targeted. They avoid you, but they laugh at me. If you get promoted to varsity practices, I know I won't be able to deal on my own."

"Fine," she gave in. "Then Neeka should talk to them."

"Me? Alone?" Neeka squeaked. "I'm not so sure."

"It kind of makes sense," Payton said. "They actually have some respect for you, since you start for varsity. You have the most authority with them. They just might listen to you."

Neeka thought about it for a second. When the warning bell rang, she gave her answer. "Okay. I'll talk to them alone. But I can't guarantee they actually will listen."

****

When Coach Mike blew his whistle to signify the end of varsity practice, Neeka winced. It was time to talk to the girls. Normally pretty outspoken, she surprised herself by how nervous she was. Leaving her bags behind, she quickly made her way down the short path to the adjoining middle school, her mind full as it tried to decide on a good way to begin the conversation.

By the time she arrived, JV had just finished practice. They came into the locker room, giggling, barely a sweat upon them.

As planned, Payton and Selina were nowhere in view. She was to meet them near the bleachers when she was finished.

That's if they don't eat me alive, Neeka worried.

"Hey, Neeka, what are you doing here?" Janette asked, happy to see her.

"Actually, I wanted to talk to you guys."

"Sure," Janette said. "Hey, everyone, over here," she shouted, motioning for the girls in the locker room to join them. "Neeka wants to talk to us."

"Us too?" one of the middle school cross-country girls asked, a smirk on her face.

"You wish!" Val said as they gathered around Neeka.

Neeka felt so awkward standing before them. She felt her hand shaking, so she quickly put it behind her back. She hoped knowing Val from basketball would make things easier. Val was their ringleader. If she showed Neeka some respect, the rest of the girls would as well.

"We in trouble?" Courtney asked.

Going mute, Neeka hesitated in replying. She knew she needed to tell them their behavior was unacceptable, but she also didn't want to tick them off to the point they wouldn't listen, as Payton had warned.

OMG, confrontation was not easy!

"Neeka?" Janette asked. "What's up?"

Taking a breath, Neeka measured her voice. She wanted to sound friendly but full of authority. "Actually, I want to know what's up with you. All of you. It's no secret there's been some division on the team. I'd even go as far as to say some bullying." She was using her mother's words.

"We're not bullies!" Val exclaimed, indignant.

Dropping her head, Janette didn't look as though she fully agreed.

"Listen, I'm not here to make accusations or point blame. I just want to know what's up. I'm your teammate too. Your feelings count to me."

"Why should we try to do our best when some of the worst players on the team are starters?" Val blurted.

"Yeah," Courtney agreed, having Val's back. "I mean, I actually have years of experience in volleyball. Maybe I wasn't as great as a hitter as I made myself out to be on the first day of practice, but I'm still pretty good. Better than others. I should be starting."

"It's so not fair," Val claimed. "Also, I'm way more talented of a *libero* than that girl on varsity. I don't care if she's a senior. I should at the very least be a sub for her. *Liberos* get injured too."

Oh. It was starting to make sense. In regard to the JV team, they were clearly referring to Payton. It didn't sound as if it was personal. They didn't hate Payton. Val just felt an injustice had been done. Neeka was ashamed to admit it, but she couldn't entirely blame the girls for feeling the way they did, but she'd never tell them that.

"But Val, you're a smart girl. Surely you can see this is not the fault of any player. None of us can do anything about where the coaches place us."

"Yes, something can be done. Those who are terrible can quit so that those who are good can start!"

Wow. She was really angry about this.

"Well, you aren't doing yourselves any favors by goofing off in practice."

Courtney spoke up again. "What's the point if we're just going to be put on the bench?"

Neeka'd had enough. This wasn't middle school. They were in high school now. The girls couldn't expect to cry their way out of every bad situation they encountered. If Neeka was going to be their leader, she needed to teach them about responsibility.

"Listen closely. Some players are starters because they take practice seriously. Like I do. If you want more time on the court, you should do the same."

Leaving her words to ring in their ears, she stormed past them and out into the gymnasium, where Payton and Selina were waiting.

There was no way she could tell Payton what the girls had said. Even if she wanted to, she wouldn't know how. It would hurt Payton to know. Neeka was too protective of her bestie to put her through the same pain she had experienced with Annette last year.

"So, what's the verdict?" Selina asked.

"They don't think practice is important," she answered, leaving out everything Val and Courtney had said.

Payton shook her head. "Then why are they even playing in the first place? It makes no sense. I hate to say it, but I think we only have one choice left."

"What?" Neeka asked, though she knew she didn't want to hear the answer.

"We have to talk to Coach Gina."

****

"Girls, sometimes new players need more time to adjust to the unfamiliar skill sets they're learning," Coach Gina said, facing them.

They were in her office back at the high school. If they'd gone home and slept on what they had to do—confront one of their coaches—none of them would have gotten any rest that night. It was much better if they just pulled the bandaid away and got it over with. So they'd immediately gone to her office, hoping she would still be there collecting her personal things.

Neeka couldn't help but notice how she fumbled with the gold sun that hung from her neck as she spoke.

Sun. Solis.

"We're just afraid this is more about attitude and less about adaptation," Payton argued.

"I totally get that. But most of the girls have never played before. They don't yet realize that positive thinking and hard work are as much a skill as spiking."

Then teach them, like the girl in the book would, Neeka wanted to say.

"How do we teach them then?" Selina asked, in line with Neeka's thoughts.

"With patience and by setting an example. I know you girls mean well, and I appreciate you coming to me, but think about it from their perspective. They've never played before. They probably wouldn't make another team if they tried. But they were fortunate that Hickory Academy didn't hold try-outs this year. I recognize it can be frustrating at times, but our job this year isn't to turn the new girls into All-Stars overnight."

Neeka tried to speak, but Coach Gina cut her off. She continued. "This year, our job is to provide them with a positive experience so that they remain committed to volleyball. Then, next year, when they return and realize they have to fight for a place on varsity, they'll be willing to do so. Until then, I don't want to put too much pressure on them. I'll only discourage them from returning."

The conversation was over. She'd said her final words.

The girls said nothing as they filed out of the Coach Gina's office, but one thing played on all their minds. Though what Coach Gina said made sense, it wasn't enough. She simply didn't get it.

****

"Why you so glum?" Jamari asked as he drove her home from practice. "Did you talk to the girls today?"

"Unfortunately," Neeka mumbled.

He raised an eyebrow. "That bad?"

"It's Val. She's so angry that she's not on varsity and that Payton is starting over Courtney. It felt as if I was standing next to a volcano. The girl has serious issues."

"Yikes."

"Yikes is right. That's why you have to be nice to her. I don't want her crush on you to cause even more trouble for me on JV."

"I like my women to have a little killer instinct, but she's too backstabby for me," he quipped.

Neeka glared at him.

He turned at a light. "Okay, I'll go ahead and lead the godfather of JV volleyball players on. That sounds like a wonderful idea," he said sarcastically. "Let me know how that works out for you when that volcano blows up in your face."

"Thanks," Neeka mumbled.

"You know, you have another option than brown-nosing to a freshman. Coach Gina may be soft, but Coach Mike certainly isn't. Go to him."

"And say what?"

"The truth. Tell him how hardheaded the JV girls are being. I'll tell you this, you'll see their behavior correct right quick."

"But they might not make varsity next year if I do. Some of us want to win. This isn't just about the JV. We're gonna need them on the varsity."

"Nonsense. Listen, if the girls are bitter about anything Coach Mike says to them, they can't pin it on you, Payton, or rock girl. They'll only have themselves to blame. Coach Mike will make certain they understand that. It'll force them to look at their own behavior."

"I'm worried about varsity's future if I do," Neeka uttered.

"Yeah, but think of varsity's future if you don't."

CHAPTER 7

"Is that Papa's car in the driveway?" Neeka asked as she helped her ma clear the dishes off the dining room kitchen. "I couldn't see. The headlights were shining in my eyes."

"I certainly hope so," her ma said. "Otherwise, we're being invaded by someone who pulls into driveways and flashes their headlights at random strangers."

"Funny."

Before her ma could look, they heard the front door open and her papa bellow out, "I'm home!"

"We know!" Jamari yelled back from the kitchen. "Only you make the front door sound like a circus when you're coming in. When you going to grease that?"

"When *you* going to grease it?" her papa shot back with a smile as he entered the dining room. He scooped a piece of pasta off Neeka's plate. "Delicious. Sorry I missed." He then went and gave his wife a big kiss.

"Welcome home, Donald." Her ma affectionately placed her hand on his cheek.

"Missed ya, Mama Bear. As always."

"Yuck," Neeka said, grabbing an almost empty salad bowl to balance on top of the plates she was already carrying.

"You're home early," Jamari noted, coming in from the kitchen.

"But not early enough," her papa said regretfully as he took the plates from Neeka. "Let's leave these in the sink for now. I was thinking we could all sit down and watch TV together. It's been a while since I've been home before the kiddies went to bed."

"Kiddes?" Neeka said skeptically. "You haven't called us that in years."

"Forgive a dad for reminiscing."

"Sounds good to me, Papa," Jamari said. The boy loved TV. "But I don't have a bedtime. Not since I was sixteen."

"Yes, you do," Neeka challenged. "Only now, it's called a curfew."

Neeka had a history assignment due the next day, but it was only a simple worksheet. She could do it during study hall. Spending time with her papa was way more important. They rarely had any time with him these days. He was picking up extra shifts at the hospital, even more than normal. Her parents wouldn't say it, but Neeka knew it was because they were worried about college tuition. It was hard enough when one child went to college, but two so close together...

Neeka knew it wasn't her fault there weren't many financial aid options for middle-income parents who earned too much to qualify for government funding but not enough to pay out of pocket. The only real option was loans.

No, the history assignment could wait. Tonight, she wanted to spend time with her papa. With Jamari leaving in less than a year, there wouldn't be many opportunities for family gatherings in the future.

But as the family settled together on the coach with a large bowl of popcorn in front of them, Neeka found it hard to stay fully present. Her mind kept wondering back to the JV team. She took her team leader assignment very seriously. She'd been raised to believe hard work led to success, and she didn't understand why the JV girls didn't feel the same. She didn't know how to get through to them.

With a comedy on the screen, her parents and Jamari burst out laughing, but Neeka barely noticed. She'd missed the entire storyline. Instead, she stared blankly ahead of her, fiddling with the remote as she decided what to do.

Her papa placed a hand on her shoulder. "Honey, what's wrong?"

"Nothing," Neeka said, shaking her head. She didn't want to spoil her papa's night off.

"Clearly something is wrong."

"Tell us, Neeka," her ma prompted. "There's no better time with your father here."

Jamari groaned. "She said she was okay, so drop it. Let's just watch the TV. I can't hear it over your yapping."

"Jamari Leigh." Her ma said his name with the authority of an army general. "I did not raise a son to speak to his parents with such disrespect."

"Sorry, Ma," he said, shrinking into his shoulders.

"Neeka?" Donald probed.

"It's the JV team."

"Yes, your mother told me a little about it. What's happening?"

"There's a disconnect. The girls just want to have fun—"

Jamari broke out into the Cyndi Lauper song, but Neeka quickly shot him down with a deadly glare, so he went back to the TV show.

"They claim they don't care about winning. But they're furious Payton is starting when there are better players who aren't. So they show her no respect."

"That's terrible," Donald said. "How can they protest being treated unfairly by being unfair to someone else?"

Neeka answered, "I know!"

Jamari turned up the TV, eyeing their ma out of the corner of his eye to make sure it didn't get him into trouble.

"Well, if they're not serious about playing, they shouldn't play," her ma said matter-of-factly, ignoring her son.

"Coach Gina doesn't see it that way. We tried talking to her. She just wants the girls to stay on the team. She doesn't care if they're taking it seriously or not."

"Then get Coach Mike involved," her papa advised. "He won't put up with it."

Jamari turned the TV back down. "That's what I said." He left the volume down, his face serious.

Neeka shook her head. "Gina's not going to bench anyone, and

Coach Mike has enough to think about. He won't get involved with her business. That's why he hired her, to take the pressure off his own shoulders."

"He's head of the volleyball program at Hickory Academy. He certainly will get involved, especially if the future of the program is at stake," her papa insisted.

Jamari stepped in. "I know how hard it is, sis, to criticize a coach, especially when that coach thinks they're doing the right thing. But sometimes you have to. I was on a team once where the coach was more focused on winning than the players. He overlooked everything. None of the team had fun. So we asked an assistant coach to speak with him, and he ended up apologizing to the team."

"Really?" Neeka asked, surprised she had never heard the story before. "Or did you just make that up to help me?"

"On my captain's jersey, it's true."

"I didn't know that," her ma said, looking concerned.

Her papa kept quiet, probably having heard the story before. Neeka and Jamari loved their ma, but sometimes they went to their papa with problems they were afraid their ma would judge them too harshly on or something that would upset her too much. Her dad usually kept their problems confidential, unless the situation was beyond control.

"That's because the team solved the problem by going to someone who could help," Jamari said. "For you, sis, Coach Mike is that someone."

"I just don't feel comfortable doing that. Gina is there because of him. It feels like too much of a betrayal," she said, thinking of the book she was reading.

Jamari sat up straighter. "Then find someone else who can help."

I was never so relieved than when I heard the news that coach quit. It made my day! Freshman year of college has been hard enough without the added pressure I was feeling under the reign of Coach Leech. I call him that because that's what he does—he sucks the very spirit away from us. I swear he has a jar somewhere where he collects our souls. But I don't have to worry about that anymore! Because now he's gone. Phew.

But I can't help but feel regret over the whole thing. Not about him leaving. I'll be dancing under the moon for that! I regret that he left of his own accord after being offered a better paycheck for a university somewhere else. I would like to say at least he's their problem now, but that's not true. As long as he's out in the world hurting other volleyball players, he's still my problem. I should have reported him to a higher authority long ago, but I did nothing, too scared of losing my position on the team.

It was wrong, and now it's too late. I really should have done something. It's normal to not always get along with a coach. And trust me, diary, I've faced my share of tough coaches. I know the difference between someone who is a bad coach and someone who is just a bad person all round. Coach Leech was the second, a person who lacked all sense of human decency. The only reason he's a coach is because his father was some World Championship hotshot. I bet his father never taught him to be as nasty as he was.

Now, my thoughts turn to Courtney. She's not doing well. She's so thin! I mean, to the point people are pointing at her on the street. Whenever any of the other girls on the team try to say something to her, she tells me later that it's just because they're jealous. Why did Coach Leech have to make that stupid comment to her about her weight! It was so irresponsible. I'm literally watching my friend fade away before my eyes, and the only thing I want to do is tear the smirk off the man who did this to her. Only now, because I was too scared to, he's enjoying a promotion somewhere, and Courtney is suffering.

I hope the new coach is much better. I'm sure they will be. I don't think it's possible they can be any worse. Coach Leech doesn't have a twin, does he? That would be too much to deal with. I wonder if I can write a letter to the national volleyball authority that oversees all the college matches. You know what, diary, that's exactly what I'll do. I can't let this go!

I'm thinking about coaching one day. I've already started teaching kids at an inner city afterschool program. It's a volunteer position that requires us to tutor the kids with their homework as well as play volleyball with them, but I'm totally digging it. Get it? Digging it! I crack myself up, diary.

It's late at night. Or early in the morning, however you want to view it. I have a paper due tomorrow, but I'm going to write that letter now about Coach Leech. I don't think I can face myself in the mirror tomorrow if I don't...

As she put the book down, Neeka was thankful for one thing—

they had issues on volleyball, but nothing compared to what the author had to go through. Coach Mike was tough, but he was a really decent man, often joking with the girls when it wasn't match time. He respected them as athletes, but more so as people, even when his words were a bit harsh. She couldn't imagine a better coaching team than Coach Mike and Coach Gina.

The diary entry did help her figure out one thing. Jamari was right, yet again. She hated when that happened. The girls needed someone they could go to for help. The author of *Diary of a Young Volleyball Star* wouldn't have felt so stuck if she had someone she could trust to talk to. Thankfully, Neeka and the rest of the girls did. It wasn't Coach Mike. But it was someone who had proved very helpful in the past.

****

"We can't go to Coach Mike," Neeka said firmly.

"I don't know anyone else who can help," Selina grumbled. "Coach Mike is our only option. Unless there's such a thing as a volleyball God we can pray to."

"Well, actually—"

Suddenly, the hallways echoed with loud, obnoxious laughter. Students pointed as a giant basketball, with two arms and two legs sticking awkwardly out of it, teeter tottered its way through the crowded hallway.

"Who's that loon?" one of the kids shouted. "Did we get new school uniforms?"

Selina rubbed her eyes, smearing her mascara all over her hands. "Am I dreaming or is that a ginormous basketball walking our way?"

Instantly, Neeka remembered what she'd said to George in study hall.

Payton does not dance. Not unless it's at the end zone of a football field. If you were a basketball and she could throw you into a hoop, you might have a shot.

Oh no.

"Ummm... Payton. I think I know who it is. It's George. If you want to run, we'll cover for you."

"George?"

It was too late. George had already spotted them. Pushing his way through the remainder of the crowd, he waved at them stiffly, barely able to bend his arm in the costume.

"He looks more like a pumpkin to me," Selina noted.

"George, what's all this?" Payton asked.

To Neeka's surprise, Payton wasn't cringing. She looked thoroughly amused.

"Payton Moore," George said from the part of the costume where his cheeks poked through. With the funny accent, Neeka guessed he was trying to sound like a Knight of the Round Table, but it was all a big muffled. "My lady, would you do me the honor of escorting me to the homecoming dance?"

"George," Payton giggled. "That dance is not until mid-October. It's weeks away."

"I thought I'd get in early and ask before someone else did."

Payton patted the top of his basketball head. "I'm so sorry, George. The teachers don't usually give us much homework that weekend, so I'll likely be at my dad's in Cincinnati."

George was immediately disappointed.

"I'm sorry, George."

"It's okay," he said. "I understand. I wouldn't want to keep you from your dad." Without another word, he turned and slowly walked away.

"That is definitely the world's saddest pumpkin," Selina commented.

"I feel so bad." Payton bit her lip, watching George leave.

"Was it true what you said?" Neeka asked. "About Cincinnati?"

"Yeah. My dad and I have already talked about it."

"Then don't feel bad. There's nothing you can do," Neeka reassured her.

"So, what are we going to do about JV?" Selina asked, snapping them into attention. "Talk to Coach Mike or no?"

"I was thinking more like Dr. B," Neeka revealed.

"Dr. B?" Payton asked, surprised. "Actually, that does make sense."

Selina looked confused. "What am I missing here? Dr. B is a biology teacher. A very dorky, wears thick grandpa glasses even though he's only in his thirties, probably can't even lift a pen biology teacher. What does that have to do with volleyball?"

Neeka remained quiet. Payton's jump serve was a sensitive issue between the girls at the moment. She didn't want to bring the subject up, afraid it would rouse an argument.

Payton didn't seem to mind though. "When I was struggling last year, it was Dr. B who encouraged me to focus on one particular skill I'd be good at. I have him to thank for my jump serve. And my spot on varsity this year."

"I still don't really see how he can help us, except for telling us the same thing all our parents have said—go to Coach Mike. But we might as well see what Dr. I'm So British I Sound Like James Bond has to say."

Payton found that hilarious. "Why is it no one calls him by his real name? It's Dr. Ronald Beamon, in case you were ever wondering."

"I wasn't."

"Great, you guys are game," Neeka said. "Because I already told him we'd drop by during lunch."

✳✳✳✳✳✳✳✳✳✳✳✳✳✳✳✳✳✳

Scarfing a sandwich down as she walked toward the biology lab, Neeka felt a sense of relief. By talking to Dr. B, the burden of the issues with JV would no longer be solely on their shoulders. His advice always proved pretty wise, even if she did have a hard time understanding him sometimes with his thick British accent.

She was in a hurry to meet the girls, but she stopped halfway there when she spotted George, dressed back in his regular school uniform, taking a sip from the water fountain. His shaggy dark hair hung in his sad face, which he pushed back dejectedly. George was kooky, that was for sure, but he was actually kind of cute. And he was tall. Payton had that advantage, if she ever gave him a chance.

"That was a really sweet gesture today, George," she said when she reached him.

He look mortified to see her. "Yeah, sure. It's all cool. You don't have to make me feel better."

"You know what she said about Cincinnati was true. The situation with her parents is complicated."

"Yeah, I know." He looked away.

Her heart went out to him. "Did you ever try thinking of starting small and working your way up? Maybe nothing so dramatic?"

He faced her again, considering this. "I thought girls liked big and romantic."

Neeka pointed her finger. "Yeah, but you and I both know Payton isn't like normal girls. You probably wouldn't like her if she was."

George nodded his head. "Start small. That's hard for me. But I'll see what I can do..." As he walked away, he looked much happier. Neeka was glad. The boy was a goof, but he was genuine. He definitely had that going for him.

Payton and Selina were waiting outside the lab when she arrived.

"I still think this is weird," Selina said as they walked in.

"Ladies." Dr. B greeted them without looking up from his laptop. "If you'll excuse me for one minute, I'm just finishing an order for *drosophila melanogaster*."

"What?" Selina asked.

"Fruit flies," Neeka reminded her.

"Oh, the memories," Payton said.

A few minutes later, their former teacher clicked his laptop closed and stood. "Now, Neeka told me this morning you needed some advice. What can I do for you?" he asked in his usual soft voice.

The girls began talking all at once.

Dr. B held up a hand, quieting them. "Neeka, why don't you explain, since you called this meeting."

Neeka told him the entire story of how the JV girls were acting and how Coach Gina wasn't willing to help. She left out the part about Payton.

Dr. B rubbed his head, thinking. "And what type of actions were you hoping Coach Gina to take?"

"Tell them to shape up or they're gone," Selina answered.

"But then you would have no JV team."

"So." She shrugged her shoulders. "We're all on varsity too. We don't need JV."

Neeka sighed. "Then who is going to replace varsity as we graduate? No, threats won't work."

Dr. B agreed. "So what will?"

Payton stood on her toes, eager to talk. "We need to persuade them. Make them want to win. But they hate us. Well, me at least. So I don't know how we can do that. It's why we went to Coach Gina."

"That brings me back to my original question. What should Coach Gina be doing differently to help team chemistry and motivation at practice?"

"Everything," Selina vented, though they all knew that wasn't true. Coach Gina was a fantastic teacher when it came to instructing them on drills and improving their skills. Her only failure was the attitude adjustment the girls needed.

Neeka kept silent, thinking. It felt strange criticizing their coach in front of a teacher.

When no one else spoke, Dr. B said, "Listen. Why don't you girls have a think about what you expect from Coach Gina. Employ the scientific method. Once your objectives are clear, then take action."

The girls agreed and left the biology lab, thinking over his words.

"I'll admit, I was kind of hoping he'd go talk to the coaches for us," Selina said.

"No, that's Dr. B's style. He only meddles when he's really concerned. Otherwise, he helps you work it out on your own."

Payton put a hand over her stomach as it rumbled. "I'm starved."

"Me too. Let's get some grub," Selina said. "We have twenty minutes before lunch is over."

Neeka stopped walking. This was her chance. "Actually, I ate a sandwich on the way down. I just need to do something quickly. If there's time afterward, I'll meet ya downstairs."

"Secretive much?" Selina said, looking suspicious.

"I'll tell you about it later. Now go, eat, before Payton passes out."

"I'd argue with her, but I can't. I'm seriously hungry," Payton said.

Neeka waited until her friends were out of sight then quietly popped back into the biology lab.

Dr. B was twirling a forkful of noodles around. "Miss Leigh. What bring you back so soon?"

"There's something else I need your advice on. Something I didn't want to say in front of the other girls."

Dr. B set the fork down. "I'm listening."

"As you know from last year, Payton hasn't found volleyball too easy. She's way better than she was before. I know she spent all year practicing. And it shows. But she still has a ways to go. Some of the girls on JV... I hate to admit it, but they are equally good. They might even be better. And they know it. They show absolutely no respect toward her. Payton doesn't understand why. I can tell it's stressing her out. But I have absolutely no idea how to tell her it's because they think they're better players."

"Is Payton worried about her position on the team?"

"No. Not that I know of. We all know that no matter what, she'll still start. Once Coach Mike makes a decision, he sticks with it. I know he specifically wanted Payton to start on JV, maybe to make up for the fact he had taken her away from varsity practices."

"Then why do you feel you have to tell her?"

His question surprised her. Was he suggesting she shouldn't?

"Because she's my friend. I should be the one to tell her. I can deliver it to her gently so she doesn't find out the hard way."

Dr. B seemed pleased. "I think that is wise. Focus on Payton. Don't worry about the other girls. They will have to accept Coach Gina and Coach Mike's decision to have Payton start. It's not your responsibility to make them do so. It'll be a good life lesson for them."

So that was the final verdict. She had to tell Payton. It wouldn't be easy.

****

Varsity practice that afternoon did not go well. Neeka couldn't get Payton off her mind. Maybe if she told her over a smoothie... Or over a Dakota Fanning movie... As her mind twirled, she lost focus. During the drills, when she was meant to be setting, her timing was off, which threw the hitters off as well.

Finally, Coach Mike blew his whistle. "Leigh, get your head out of the clouds."

"Sorry, Coach," she mumbled.

"Sorry is not enough. When you step on my court, I expect you to leave all your worries outside. The only thing on your mind should be the game. This isn't a therapy session. This is high school championship volleyball."

And who do you think helped turn this team into champions? she thought, but kept it to herself.

However, Coach Mike didn't miss the snarky look on her face. "Knox, you take over Leigh's place as setter. Leigh, sit on the bench. Watch what happens to your varsity position when you stop playing for the team."

Lacey glanced at Neeka apologetically as they passed each other on the court.

It's okay, Neeka mouthed.

But the truth was, it wasn't. Because at the end of the day, she still had to tell Payton the truth.

CHAPTER 8

It was another boring old evening trapped inside her house. Payton didn't know what to do with herself. She still had her full allowance for the week, but Neeka's family had a scheduled Skype call with her grandma in Georgia, so she was stuck at home. Selina was taking driving lessons, not that Payton would automatically call her, still sore about the jump serve issue. Payton had other friends, but they moved around so quickly, it was impossible to keep in touch with them without a mobile phone. They could be in a restaurant one minute and gone the next.

No longer able to stare at the walls of her bedroom, Payton ran downstairs, deciding to do something about her situation. "Mom!" she hollered. "I really think we need to discuss the phone issue again."

Allison met her at the stairs. "I told you already, no phones or dating until you're sixteen."

"But that's only a few months away," she whined. "I promise not to date until I'm seventeen if you get me a phone now."

Tempted, her mom almost considered this, then stopped. "No, Payton. Rules are rules for a reason."

She moved to the front room and plopped on the couch. "I can't wait until I'm sixteen."

Her mom followed her in. "Don't try to grow up too fast. You know what also happens when you're sixteen? You're old enough to get a job."

Her mom was joking, right? "We have loads of money. Why would I have to work?"

Her mom straightened her skirt, a habit of hers when she was about to talk about something that either bothered her or was important to her. "Payton, I was not always a successful interior designer. I had to work my way up from the bottom. My parents were like Neeka's—comfortable but certainly not rich. I had to get a job at sixteen. And then I had to take out loans when I wanted to start the business. I fought for everything I have."

Payton listened, captivated. Her mom rarely revealed this side of her past. "I'm still not sure what that means. Do I have to get a job?"

Allison sat next to her. "Not now, but yes, at some point in the next year or two. I think a job teaches really good values, like financial responsibility, and it looks good on college applications."

She looked around their big house almost regrettably. "Maybe I'm wrong, but if I'm being completely honest, I tend to think those with less money have stronger family units. My parents did. And so do Neeka's family."

Payton placed her hand on top of her mom's. "Hey, we're a strong family unit."

"Yes, we are. I'm going to miss you when you go off to college, that's all."

"Don't worry, who do you think I'm going to bring my laundry home to every Sunday?" Payton joked.

Her mom rolled her eyes then changed the subject. "Payton, my darling daughter, seeing that you are almost sixteen, I thought we could do something with your room."

Not this same old story again. Payton jumped up, suddenly losing interest, and tried to hit the bottom of the chandelier hanging from the high vaulted ceiling.

"Don't do that, you'll unhitch the wiring," her mom warned.

"Yes, modder," she said, impersonating a small child.

"So, your room?"

"Gonna stay the same. Give it up, Mom. This is the 20th century. Girls like sports memorabilia too." Her room was essentially a shrine to the Titans.

"Firstly, Payton, this is the 21st century, not the 20th century, and I find nothing wrong with the sports gear. It's just an eyesore with all the clashing colors and bland textures."

Payton stopped listening. Her mother was always looking for a new project. After her parents had split and her dad moved out, her mom had redecorated the entire house. The only room left untouched was Payton's, but there was no way she was going to change it. It was the only thing she had left of her former life when she had happily married parents and a dad who coached her nightly. Plus, it was her, through and through. Who didn't want to snuggle into a big ole Titans comforter at night?

In fact, when I move out, I'm making my mom sing a contract that she won't change my room, Payton decided.

Bored again, Payton lumbered down into the basement game room to practice her table tennis against the back wall. But just as she was really getting into the game, her mom called down the stairs, "Payton, Neeka's on the phone."

Happy for something to do, Payton raced upstairs to her bedroom and snatched her hot dog shaped phone up. "What's up, jelly bean?"

"I need to talk to you." Neeka sounded concerned.

Payton twisted the phone cord around her hand, nervous at Neeka's tone of voice. "Is everything okay?"

"Yes and no," Neeka said then launched into what she had to say. "I wasn't entirely truthful to you and Selina about what the JV girls said to me. But Team Scary Pancake won't be able to move forward with our plans unless you know the whole story. The reason they don't find practice important is because they think it's useless to try. They're not too happy about the fact that you start when Courtney doesn't. They don't think it's fair."

Payton said nothing at first, digesting what Neeka told her. The words were a shock to hear, at first, but the more Payton thought about it, the more it made sense. She had accepted long ago that she wouldn't be the best volleyball player in town. She was working hard to improve.

But that didn't change the fact that Courtney was a much better hitter with several years more experience than Payton. Still, she didn't start.

If Payton were in her shoes, she'd probably feel exactly the same.

"Payton?" Neeka said gently. "Are you okay? You're not crying, are you? I can ask Ma if I can come over."

Appreciating Neeka's concern but finding it amusing, she laughed. "No, silly. I'm not crying. I totally get it. I tried to lead by example and that obviously didn't work. And now I know why. In a way, it's a relief."

"So I did the right thing by telling?" Neeka sounded much more relaxed.

"Yeah, you did, jelly bean. I can't blame the freshmen for feeling the way they do. I'm not the best on the team, so why would they follow my lead?"

"But they still need to recognize it's not your fault. They need to accept things are the way they are. It's no excuse for them to be behaving like this."

"True, but now we have something to work with. We know why they're so moody. They don't feel appreciated, so they have no loyalty to the team. Or us."

Payton heard Neeka snap her fingers near the phone. "So all we have to do is let them know how much they are appreciated. Then they'll be more committed and want to do well. Coach Gina keeps her JV squad intact. And we start winning!" She sounded excited.

"Geesh, after all this, maybe it would have been easier to go all Annette and fry their bacon instead of playing nice."

"Yeah," Neeka said. "There's no way Val would have started this whole campaign if you gave her one of Annette's icy stares, the one she did when we were losing."

"Do you remember the look she gave you after we lost Sub-State last year?" Payton felt a shiver go down her spine. "I'll never forget it."

The girls burst out laughing.

"If Annette were still here, I think Coach Gina's worst fears would come true," Payton predicted. "All you'd see in the middle school gym is a few volleyballs lying around a dusty floor. We have to stick to our pact that we'll never go all Annette."

"Of course," Neeka said, but she thought she heard hesitation in her friend's voice.

****

"Great job, Val!" Payton praised, working her inner Coach Gina instead of her inner Annette. "The varsity *libero* better watch out!"

For the first time in weeks, Val smiled at her. Not one of her fake "I'm going to smile now and then talk about you behind your back" smiles. But a real, genuine smile, almost to the point where it was bashful.

"Thanks," she said. "I've been practicing that move at home all week."

That's a good sign, Payton thought.

Initiating their plan to make the freshmen feel more appreciated, Team Scary Pancake had driven their energy into pointing out the girls' strengths, giving them encouragement, making them feel they were just as talented as the varsity girls.

Payton was starting to understand Coach Gina's tactics more and more, but she still didn't feel that was an excuse to let the JV behavior slide so easily this season. One of the biggest lessons athletics were meant to teach was teammanship and discipline. She'd been on enough losing and winning teams to know that.

Now that the secret of why the JV didn't seem to care was out, and Team Scary Pancake was working to rectify things, JV practices were bearable again, though far from the happiness she felt when playing on varsity. But overall, Payton felt much lighter knowing she hadn't been targeted for personal reasons, just the injustice the girls thought had occurred.

Ending the current drill, Coach Gina called them over to join her near the net to begin another. "I really want to sharpen your skills," she informed them. "I see so much potential in all of you. I hope you all realize the talent you have. Now we just need to take that talent and improve—"

"Is that a bird at the top of the bleachers?" Val asked, pointing to where a black lump laid.

"It's just one of those pencil cases art students like me carry around," Selina told her. "I have one similar."

"No, I think it's a bird," Val insisted. "I'm going to check it out."

Coach Gina put her hands on her hips. "I really don't think it's necessary."

But Val was determined. Ignoring the protests of her coach, she leapt up the steps of the bleachers to the black blob. With nothing else to do, the team watched her, waiting until she came back down.

She shook the object in the air. "You were right, Selina, it's a pencil case. But at least now you can give it back to the owner. We can't say JV didn't do a good deed today." She handed Selina the case, who slid it on the floor toward the back wall.

"Well done, Val. I'm sure that student will be very pleased," Coach Gina praised.

It took all of Payton's control not to roll her eyes.

"Now, ladies, I really see a lot of potential in each of you. But we have to bring that talent forward so that the rest of the district can see it too. You're each a hidden gem. With a little polish, you can shine on the court." Val and a few of the girls snickered, but Coach Gina continued, not at all fazed.

Maybe Coach Gina was such a good volleyball player, she learned to drown out all background noise, even when she's not playing. It would explain a lot.

"We have a match against Demonbreun High coming up. I guarantee you, it will be tough. Demonbreun High has a mean offense, but so can we, if we practice. I know we're still working on a few of your positions on the team, especially with the new freshmen. Every day, we discover the talents you have hidden within. Some of you are great hitters or blockers, others both. A good few of you dominate the back row. But for today, we're all hitters."

Courtney raised her hand, hopeful. "Does this mean the starting line-up might change?"

"There are no plans to, not yet. Those who are starting will continue to start, while those who are subbing will continue to sub, but as the season progresses, we might switch your positions up a bit, depending on where your strengths and weaknesses are. It'll be fun! We all like to try something new, right?"

"Not me," Val muttered. "I'm a *libero*, and I'm staying a *libero*."

"At least you're starting," Courtney hissed, loud enough for Payton to hear.

Coach Gina held the ball up high with one hand. "The entire game of volleyball revolves around this. It's kind of strange when you think about it. The jerseys we wear, the type of court we use, the equipment we buy, it all comes down to this ball. Careers are made with this ball, as are dreams. Ironically, the one thing you have to remember about this ball is that it's your enemy."

"Dramatic much?" Val whispered to the girls around her, quietly enough that her words didn't reach Coach Gina's ears.

"The entire objective of volleyball is to get this ball away from your team, but not chaotically so. You have to make sure it never comes back. The only way to do that is to attack and attack strong. Within the few seconds that the ball is in your possession, you have to figure out the weaknesses of the other team, use that information to decide where to send the ball, and then aim with precision. It's not an easy thing to do. You can look at things like body language and routine, but you can never really know what the other team is thinking."

Coach Gina put the ball down. "We won't worry about all that today. That's something to work toward during your journey within the Hickory Academy volleyball program. Today, we're simply going to concentrate on aim."

From her back pocket, she pulled out thick red tape then walked over to the other side the net and formed several large X's on the floor. "With Janette setting, I want you to work on hitting at least one of these targets."

"Easy," Courtney said, pushing her way forward. "I'll go first."

The girls quickly lined up behind her while Janette took her position near the net to set. Within seconds of her releasing the ball, Courtney was on it. Jumping high in the air, the girl slammed it over, hitting the middle target dead center.

"Kill shot!" Coach Gina cheered.

"You're almost as good as I am," Selina shouted. It was the closest Selina got to a compliment, especially when the competition was involved.

Courtney read it for what it was. Her eyes lit up. "Glad you enjoyed the show."

At this rate, we might actually start winning some matches, Payton thought happily. *I'd hate it if we went through the entire season without winning a single match.*

At least varsity was doing well. They dominated their district, beating out the Vikings, Hawks, and other prominent teams. But they had yet to face their arch rivals—Demonbreun High. That match was in a few days. Already, the hallways of the high school were decked out in banners and cut-out volleyballs. There had even been an announcement about it in the sports section of the local paper. It was a highly anticipated match.

Only two days to go....

****

Sweat stung her eyes as Payton lifted the ball, preparing to serve. She could barely see the jam-packed gymnasium that surrounded her, but that didn't matter. She shut out the noise—the cheers, the chatter. From the bench, she'd studied the Demonbreun High girls carefully. Like most teams, when they ran into formation after the serve, they favored the left side of the court.

She knew that the player who would move into the right back corner was their weakest. When the girl had the ball, she could pass it with ease to their setter. But when the ball came toward her hard and low, with a bit of spin, she had difficulty recovering it.

So that was precisely the serve Payton would deliver.

Jumping high in the air, she sent the ball spiraling toward her target.

Point.

As Payton reclaimed the ball to serve again, the Demonbreun High coach signaled to the back row, no doubt telling her *libero* to cover the girl. If Payton was correct, this would leave a section of the court in the middle, toward the left, free. Trusting her instincts, she served.

Point.

Coach Mike punched his hand into the air. "Eagle eyes, Payton. That's the way to play."

The score had been close, but now Hickory Academy was far in the lead in the fifth set. As usual, Coach Mike had saved her for the end so that she could close out the match, taking the pressure of her fellow teammates, who were growing tired after a hard fought battle.

Not the same as starting, but I'll take it, for now.

Payton served again. It was flawless. The Demonbreun High defense didn't stand a chance.

On both sides, a gasp came from the bleachers.

The fans were used to seeing her serve, yet she still managed to impress. It gave her endless satisfaction knowing that. She smiled, proud.

By the time Demonbreun High was finally able to return her serve and score a point, Hickory Academy was only one point away from the winning fifteen. It was very unlikely Demonbreun High would catch up.

Coach Mike signaled for her to come back to the bench. "My secret weapon," he said, patting her on the back. "Though you're not so secret anymore."

It was an enormous compliment coming from Coach Mike, but as Payton watched Selina out on the court, knowing the girl had been given much more playing time, Payton couldn't help but feel jealous. Being a secret weapon wasn't enough. She wanted to start, and then grow into an All-Star. She'd fooled herself to believe she accepted things as they were, but truly, she couldn't ignore her desire to be the best.

Some part of her still hoped that her natural athleticism would kick in, causing her to be phenomenal.

As she watched her teammates, studying them with the same intensity as their rivals, she knew that her jealousy made her a terrible leader. She wasn't setting a good example.

But in that moment, she didn't care.

CHAPTER 9

In the biology lab, there was an assortment of trays and scalpels carefully situated on the tables, no doubt in some sort of logistical order, knowing Dr. B. A projector in the middle of the classroom propelled the image of a frog's anatomy onto the whiteboard. Arrows drawn with blue marker pointed to the main organs of the amphibian.

"Ugg, don't tell me you're dissecting frogs," Payton said with disgust.

"The frogs died naturally," Dr. B said softly as he adjusted the projector, trying to make the image clearer. "I did not get them from a biology supply company. I sourced them from a local breeder who usually sells live frogs to pet stores. But sometimes viruses spread around the populations. He freezes the carcasses to donate to schools, like Hickory Academy, who are looking for more ethically sourced frogs to dissect. No money is exchanged. It's all air tight."

His speech sounded practiced. He'd probably prepared it as a pre-emptive measure to any questions the students had. Dr. B was always prepared.

"Doesn't make it any less disgusting." Payton gagged as the image on the whiteboard become totally clear. "Why didn't we do this last year? I'm glad we didn't, don't get me wrong, but I'm curious."

"Due to protests, the Hickory Academy Board of Directors decided against dissection several years ago. But I always believed science was meant to be hands on. Last spring, I heard about the breeder by word of mouth and investigated, then sent a petition onto the board. Since I was able to source the carcasses naturally and by donation, students now have the option of dissection. They can sit out without consequence if they choose to."

One thing about Dr. B she always liked was that he was straightforward in the way he spoke with the students. He didn't treat them like kids by talking in patronizing tones. To him, they were equivalent to adults. Everything he said was matter-of-fact.

"Then I'm glad I came to school extra early to talk to you, before the lab gets covered in guts and blood."

Stepping away from the projector, Dr. B insisted she have a seat in the chair in front of his desk. "So what's on your mind?" he asked, his voice as monotone as ever. But she knew it wasn't a reflection of Dr. B's character. He cared very much about all his students.

"I don't have a right to be a leader on the JV team. At least, I don't feel like one."

Dr. B didn't blink. "And why would you say that?"

Payton didn't want to admit the truth out loud. She knew how horrible it sounded. But she had to. "I'm jealous of Selina and Neeka. They get way more playing time than I do. I want to start for varsity."

"That is the nature of athletics—to compete, sometimes even against your friends and teammates. I don't understand how that makes you a terrible leader."

Payton thought it was obvious. "Because it's wrong to be jealous of your friends and teammates. I'm setting a horrible example."

"Do you act out on this jealousy? Do you ignore Selina or gossip about Neeka?"

"Of course not." Payton was insulted he would ask. "I have my moments with Selina, but I would never intentionally try to hurt anyone."

"Then that makes you an even stronger leader," he declared. "If you think you, or anyone else, will go through their entire life without being jealous of others from time to time, you're fooling yourself. Being a role model isn't about denying your emotions. It's about handling them in a responsible manner. It's only natural you might feel jealous. But the fact that you're not acting out on it in any other way than trying to improve your performance on the court says a lot about your character and your leadership abilities."

It seemed sensible, but she had other issues. "What about the JV girls? They don't take me seriously at all. Usually, leaders are upperclassmen or the best players on the team. I'm neither, not even with my jump serve."

"Sometimes being a leader is what you do behind the scenes. You brought a problem to your coach with the best intentions for the team in mind. That couldn't have been easy. You were chosen for a reason, Payton. Don't doubt yourself so casually."

"I know why the coaches selected me. They appreciate my hard work. But that doesn't matter to the JV team. I can't lead if I'm not respected."

Dr. B folded his hands. "But you are respected. The varsity team respects you. Why do you think that is?"

Payton was dumbstruck. His question caught her off guard. Until he pointed it out, she'd never realized the varsity team respected her. But it was true. They did. But why?

"I have no idea," she answered honestly.

****

A drizzly October haze covered the grounds of Hickory Academy. In their usual spot under the willow tree, Team Scary Pancake sat with Lacey, conversing about volleyball. But today, instead of the scorching heat, they were taking shelter from the warm raindrops that sprinkled around them.

Lacey lay on her stomach with a college application in front of her. It saddened Payton, knowing this was the last season they'd play volleyball with her. She couldn't imagine the team without Lacey. She was their rock, the person that brought them back to center.

Her chat earlier with Dr. B had helped her realize that perhaps she did have the potential to be an okay leader to the JV girls. But it hadn't changed the insecurity she felt toward her role on varsity, especially when it came to Selina. She still felt threatened that, if Selina perfected her jump serve, Coach Mike would have found a new secret weapon, and Payton would be replaced entirely.

"How beautiful is this?" Neeka asked, then read out a passage from her book.

I saw snow glistening on the mountain today. I couldn't take my eyes off it. It called to me, the way the bay does during the summer or the hillsides in the fall. I quickly collected the girls in my SUV and drove them up the mountain for an impromptu game of snow volleyball. It was entirely impossible! We couldn't move, not even in the thinnest of layers. But that made it all the more fun. I don't think we've ever laughed like that, not as a team. What a difference a new coach can make. We feel so relaxed. We're finally able to enjoy ourselves.

I get it now, the meaning of it all. We can't play forever. Eventually, our joints will grow old, followed by our bodies. And then we'll return to the land, return to the snow. But until then, we have sports like volleyball to give us purpose and unite us, helping us to see the connection we share with everything else around us. I'm not Captain, not yet, but knowing this, I do feel it my responsibility to make sure my fellow teammates understand that the point of volleyball isn't to win. It's simply to play.

"That is quite poetic," Lacey said. "I might borrow that book off you when you're finished."

Payton wondered if Lacey knew Neeka's theory that Coach Gina was the author. They'd vowed not to say it to anyone, just in case, even though Payton found the possibility highly unlikely. But listening to the words, she found herself drawn to the book, just like Lacey, no matter who the author was.

"Speaking of captains, who is Captain of the varsity team?" Selina asked. "I thought Coach Mike would have chosen one by now."

Lacey was confused. "Didn't he make that clear in our meetings over the summer? This whole team leadership thing is a trial run, an experiment if you will, to see if a few team leaders work better than one specific captain."

"That must be why Coach Gina never put who would be JV Captain to a vote," Neeka deciphered.

"It's ridiculous," Selina pouted. "What if all the team leaders want something different? The girls need one authority figure to turn to."

"That's what a coach is for," Neeka said.

"I actually had a talk with Dr. B on our responsibilities as leaders," Payton admitted. "I'm a little worried that I'm not a great leader when it comes to the JV girls," she said, feeling like a hypocrite with Selina sitting next to her.

"That's insane," Neeka protested. "It's not your fault they feel the way they do."

"It kind of is," Payton objected.

"No," Lacey said firmly, sounding like a mother hen. "It isn't. Coach Mike and Coach Gina knew what they were doing when they gave you three leadership roles. You're only sophomores and new to volleyball yourselves. All of you have skills you need to work on. You're still growing as players. But the coaches weren't interested in your level of play, not when it came to choosing you to help lead the teams. They chose you because you care about the volleyball program at Hickory Academy as much as they do. Payton, you proved it last year by not giving up, by pushing yourself to improve as best you could. That is exactly the kind of example the coaches want set for the younger girls."

Lacey sighed, tucking her college application away before she continued. "This program is only in its fourth year. Varsity is doing well, but greatness isn't defined by one season. It takes many championship seasons for a school to be great. Otherwise, you're just a one-hit wonder. We all have worked way too hard to be a one-hit wonder. When I return to this school ten years from now, I want to see a display case full of trophies. And in the middle, I want to see a team photo of me standing next to all y'all. And I want to see a long line of team photos underneath it. I want to stare at that display case and know I helped start the legacy—that I helped make it happen."

Payton closed her eyes. As Lacey spoke, she pictured herself ten years older, hopefully still playing for the WNBA, returning to Hickory

Academy for their reunion, gazing across the photos and trophies.

And finally, she got it. Her spot on the volleyball team wasn't about her alone. It was about something much bigger.

****

That afternoon, with the District Championship fast approaching and varsity heading into the remainder of the season undefeated, Coach Mike asked Selina and Payton to join varsity practice. There was too much at stake not to keep them close. They may be substitutes, but they were still varsity.

"Welcome back," Lacey greeted her as she emerged from the changing room.

At that moment, a hard dose of reality hit Payton. This whole time, Team Scary Pancake had assumed that neither she nor Selina would lose their spot as starters on the JV team, no matter how unfair the JV girls thought it was. But Lacey had been removed from the starting line-up last year when Coach Mike saw what a well-rounded player and exceptional setter Neeka was. If Lacey could be benched, so could the rest of them. Nothing was set in stone.

"Did I say something wrong?" Lacey asked. "You've gone all pale."

"Of course not," Payton said. "I just got lost in thought."

Coach Mike blew the whistle for practice to start and told them to stand in a circle on the court.

"Who's the best hitter we have?" he asked.

After a pause, one of the seniors raised her hand half-heartedly, afraid it was a trick question. They all were. Coach Mike didn't ask. He told.

"Good. You've just volunteered. No matter how great we are on the offense, there will be some hits that are impossible to reach. You need to know how to recognize an oncoming kill shot, and you need to know how to block it. She," he pointed to the senior, "is your number one enemy this afternoon. Lacey, you'll set for her."

With Lacey and the hitter on one side of the net, the rest of the girls positioned themselves on the other side, their main task to block the shots coming at them.

Payton looked over at Selina next to her. With her height a major advantage, blocking was one of Payton's strong points. She could easily out-show Selina, try to prove she was more than a one-hit wonder. That she had other skills she was strong at.

But Lacey's words from lunch were engrained within her heart. She was part of the Hickory Academy volleyball tradition. She had to think of the team, not just herself.

It was hard—really, really hard—but as the ball was fired across the net toward them, instead of working against Selina, Payton tried to work with her. Soon, the pair built a steady rhythm. Selina shook the net, clearly fired up. It surprised Payton, and she began to feel just as excited at what they were accomplishing together.

They were meant to return to the back of the line once they missed a block, but it wasn't happening anytime soon. Tiring the senior's arm out, Coach Mike switched her with another hitter, and still Selina and her continued to block every attack.

Around them, the rest of the team began to cheer.

"I guess sophomores have more fun!" Coach Mike yelled.

"I guess we do," Payton said.

****

"There's my brother now," Neeka said as Jamari's orange jeep pulled into the parking lot. "Thank God we're nowhere near the middle school gym. I can't put up with any more of Val flirting with my brother."

"You insisted he play along," Payton recapped.

Neeka dropped her head. "I know. Don't remind me."

"I hope I never have to go back to JV," Payton said. "Varsity was so much fun today. I know we have our own arguments now and again, but for the most part, we all get on so well. This is what I hoped JV would be like, but nothing we do seems to be working."

Neeka looked hopeful. "Things still might change."

"I don't see how. We've literally done everything we can. We encourage our fellow JV players so that they feel appreciated. We've talked to Coach Gina. We've even gone to Dr. B. What more can we possibly do?"

"I don't know," Neeka confessed. "But we can't give up. There's a solution to every problem. We just have to find it. If we don't, next year's varsity team isn't going to be nearly as good as it is this year. JV hasn't even won a match. These are the girls that will be taking over the seniors' places. We're team leaders. We have to look after the future of this program, just like Lacey said."

As soon as Jamari pulled up, Neeka opened the back door closest to them. "We're taking Payton home today. Her mom is working."

"Gladly," Jamari said, smiling. "Hop in, adopted sis."

Suddenly, his eyes darted to the gym doors where Lacey walked out wearing a pair of skinny jeans, a long T-shirt, and oversized sneakers. Jamari watched her as she lugged her equipment bag to her car, a silly grin playing on his lips.

"Don't even think about it," Neeka warned, slapping him lightly across the head.

Payton smiled. She actually thought they'd make a cute couple. She was Team Jacey.

Jamari started the car. "You can't stop true love, sis," he said, glancing at Lacey one last time before they drove away from the school. "I've been kissed by cupid."

"More like kissed by stupid," Neeka mumbled. "Please, Jamari, whatever you do, don't make Val mad. We have enough problems on JV as it is."

"When I agreed to play along, I thought you meant just be nice to her. Say hello and all that. But now she corners me at everyone one of your matches. Enough is enough. It's only going to hurt her feelings in the end."

Neeka said nothing, knowing he was right.

"JV practices are going better," Payton said, making conversation in the awkward silence that followed. "The chemistry is still way off and the girls still goof around, but they seem to be showing more commitment to the team. I'm pretty sure most are coming back next year."

"That's great," Jamari said.

Neeka stretched her arms up. "Not really. Their attitude still stinks. And we're still losing. Even if they do come back next year, it'll likely be a terrible season for varsity and JV."

"Did you talk to Coach Mike like I suggested?"

"No. We talked to a teacher. He gave us good advice. We realized the girls needed to feel more appreciated."

"But you guys still haven't gelled completely?" Jamari probed.

"No," they both answered.

"Then don't think about next year. Focus on now, this year. You still have almost half a season to get through. If not Coach Mike, I really think you should go back to Coach Gina. Try to readdress the issues. Be brutal. Leave nothing out."

"She'll only say the same thing, that she doesn't want to discourage the team," Neeka said. "Won't she, Payton?"

Usually, Payton agreed with Neeka. But this time, she thought Jamari had a point. "Actually, I agree with your brother."

"Our brother," Jamari corrected her. "You're family too. Not by blood, but once you've seen Papa belch after a meal and Ma scream at him, you're in."

Payton laughed. "Okay, I agree with *our* brother. Last time we went to Coach Gina, all we did was point out the girls' behavior. We didn't tell her why the girls were acting the way they were. Now we can."

Neeka shook her head. "What if she suddenly agrees with them and pulls you off the starting line-up? I didn't think it was possible, but Coach Mike threatened me the other day. Are you willing to risk that?"

"Of course," Payton said brightly, even though her stomach lurched at the idea. "It's for the team."

CHAPTER 10

Under a full moon, Payton went outside to shoot some hoops. It was late, but she couldn't sleep. Her mom didn't mind, not as long as she didn't leave the yard. Those were the rules of her curfew. She had to be back home by a certain time, depending on whether it was a school day or weekend, but the driveway counted as home.

Right now, home was exactly where Payton wanted to be.

The girls had decided to talk to Coach Gina the following afternoon. To say she was nervous would be an understatement. She knew she risked losing her spot on the team. Even if things went well with Coach Gina, there was still the possibility this was as far as she was ever going to get in her volleyball career. Courtney was proving to be an excellent hitter, and Selina had always been better than her. Plus there were the juniors ahead of them who, next year, would be seniors.

Might as well start training for basketball now, she thought. *It may be all I have left.*

Frustrated, she missed an easy shot. The ball bounced off the backboard, landing in the shrubs that surrounded their driveway. Payton pulled it out, scraping her hands on thorns as she did.

A light in the window above came on. Her mom waved down at her then drew the curtains closed.

Watching the curtains close did something to her. She sat on top of the ball, feeling tears come to her eyes. Payton liked basketball. She liked every sport she played. But her passion for volleyball was different. She'd spent a lot of time practicing her volleyball skills. Fighting for her place on the volleyball team, knowing she had worked hard to be there, felt just as good as making the All-Star team in basketball.

Now, she could lose it all. Next year she'd be a junior. It was rare that a junior played for anything except varsity, but it wasn't unheard of. Even if Courtney and Selina beat her to varsity, she would probably still have a spot on JV. But it would be unlikely that Neeka and Selina would play both teams again. She'd be left alone. And then, when her senior year came, and varsity was her only option, if Hickory Academy finally held try-outs, she'd be out for good.

She'd tried out for teams before, but she'd always been selected. Having been the best at everything athletic, she had never had to confront the fear of really wanting something but also knowing it might be denied to her because of her lack of skills. She thought back to all the times she'd seen girls crying in the hallway because they hadn't made the cheerleading squad or boys punching in their lockers because they'd been cut from football.

If passion were skill, she'd be on the starting line-up of varsity now. But that wasn't the way it worked. Some passions were only meant to live on as dreams.

Payton looked up, letting the tears flow. She rarely cried, so might as well get it all out of her system now. Above her, the stars twinkled knowingly. She could see why Neeka was so fascinated with them. They were a source of comfort.

Neeka.

Sniffling, Payton realized Neeka was probably going through the same thing, thinking ahead to basketball. As freshmen, they'd pretty much known last year that they were destined for the JV team. But this year was different. They could end up in any direction. Neeka definitely preferred volleyball over basketball. It was hard for her not to given her mad volleyball skills, but Payton knew her friend still enjoyed basketball. She'd dedicated so many years of her life to it. She'd want to continue playing.

But they had to try-out. And Neeka wasn't exactly the best.

On the stars, Payton made a vow that she would do everything she could to help Neeka with basketball try-outs, even if it meant overlapping her volleyball training with time under the hoop with her friend. They didn't have to go through the fear of the unknown alone.

After all, what was a bestie if not a battle companion?

****

"I kind of feel like we're cornering her," Payton said as Team Scary Pancake walked toward Coach Gina's office. They were already in their varsity practice clothes, having changed in the bathroom before their last period, a tradition that was becoming more and more frequent for Hickory Academy volleyball. They didn't want to be late for varsity practice, but they knew this took precedence. A quick chat, and then they'd run to the gym.

"Well, we're not cornering her," Selina said. "We can't just wait around for her to come to us. As long as we play it smooth, we'll be fine."

The hallways of Hickory Academy were empty. A pleasant Thursday afternoon, the student body had scattered the minute the bell rang, releasing them. The only souls left walking the halls were the athletes with practice that afternoon.

"To think," Payton said. "If I hadn't joined volleyball, I'd probably be heading to the small gym for table tennis right now."

Neeka contemplated this. "I'd be at home waiting for basketball to start."

"Am I the only one who wasn't coerced into v-ball?" Selina asked.

"Yes," Neeka and Payton said.

They'd hoped to catch her in her office, but just then Coach Gina came around the corner, walking down the hallway, heading toward JV practice. She carried a notepad in her hand, along with an inflatable beach ball.

"What's the beach ball for?" Selina whispered.

"Some drill," Neeka said. "We did it last year. You were out sick that practice."

And I was at varsity practice, not JV, Payton thought. *Things really have flipped.*

"Coach Gina!" Neeka called out.

The woman smiled as they met in the hallway. "Girls, how are you? Shouldn't you be getting ready for varsity practice?"

"We wanted to talk with you first," Neeka explained.

"Okay, walk and talk with me," Gina said pleasantly. "Are you still concerned about the motivation of the JV girls?"

"Yes," Payton admitted, "but not for the reason you think."

She felt she should be the one to explain. After crying her tears the night before and letting her emotions fall out of her, her more practical side had kicked in. She really didn't think today was the end for her. Maybe next year or the year after, but not now. Yes, Coach Mike might one day pull her off varsity, the way he had Lacey the starting line-up, but his decisions were always his own. Neither he nor Coach Gina would let some freshie JV players decide for them.

"You see, the JV girls don't think it's fair that I'm starting and Courtney isn't, even though Courtney is equally as good as me, if not better."

Unlike last time, Coach Gina frowned, concerned as she listened to Payton speak.

"That's why the chemistry is so off. They resent me. So they ignore me and goof off at practice. I think it gives them some false sense of control. They like playing volleyball, but they don't like the way the ship is run."

Coach Gina started to reply, but Neeka quickly added, "We're not here to complain. We want to fix the problem. We're concerned if we don't, the girls won't be ready for the next level. They need to see their place within the team. Otherwise, they won't fit in with varsity next year."

"Those frosh are playing volleyball for Hickory Academy. They're helping shape the program. We want them to realize how significant that is," Selina put in.

By the time they were finished speaking, they were halfway down the path to the middle school. Coach Gina stopped, taking a minute to collect her thoughts.

Payton studied her face. She didn't look angry, just troubled. A faraway look took hold of the woman's expression, as if she were reliving a memory buried deep within her.

Finally, she spoke, walking as she did. "I didn't realize the girls were being disrespectful or that the chemistry was so off. I knew there was a lack of motivation, but I didn't feel it needed tackling, for reasons I gave you before, but also because I saw how much the girls have been progressing. I was proud of them for that. Proud of all of you. But now I realize that we could have progressed a lot further."

"What should we do?" Neeka asked as they reached the gymnasium doors.

"I want the three of you to address your concerns to the girls at practice. But I'll speak first."

What! Payton had not been expecting that. She hated confrontation. Even with one person, it felt like standing in front of a firing squad. This would be a whole group of girls, ones who already had a distaste for her. She feared the freshmen would resent her even more for it.

Goodbye any hope of me being friends with JV, she thought as they opened the doors.

****

The girls slowly trickled out of the locker room one by one. JV practices usually always started late. The girls weren't exactly punctual, especially not when Val had a story to tell them. Payton had lost count of the number of times she and Selina had sat by themselves in the gym while they waited for their teammates to join them.

As expected, Val was the last to arrive. "What's going on here?"

she asked. "This a pow wow or something?"

The other JV girls were sitting on the floor, facing Coach Gina while Team Scary Pancake sat on the bleaches behind them.

"Take a seat on the floor," Coach Gina instructed her. "We're having a family meeting."

Courtney patted the empty floor next to her. "Sit here, Val."

Payton glanced nervously at Neeka. *What do you think she's going to say?* she mouthed.

Neeka shrugged her shoulders, just as anxious.

Without any further delay, Coach Gina jumped in. "I know there have been questions about why some players start over others. And while I completely understand those concerns, when you're playing on a team, you do not take your frustrations out on a fellow teammate. We can't disrespect each other anymore. It's my fault. I let things go too far for too long."

She started pacing in front of the girls. "One of my former coaches was a crazy dictator, to put it nicely. He liked getting in the player's heads, using intimidation as a motivational technique. But it was counterproductive. No one wants to play if they don't feel loyal to their team or coach. We were so afraid of him, we started screwing up. We lost our ability to encourage each other. We got down on each other instead of trying to lift each other up."

Next to her, Neeka looked almost excited listening to the story.

"When I became a coach, I swore I'd never be like him. I haven't been. And I'm proud of that. But I forgot that, like everything in life, there's a balance. I've been too lenient with you girls. As a result, I've failed to teach an important life lesson: dedication. Sometimes in life, you have to fight for what you love. By fight, I mean work hard and stay committed. If you're not willing to do that for an activity you're heavily involved in, like volleyball, then it's probably not something you should be spending your time doing."

She paused, letting her words sink in. "So no more disrespecting other players on the team. No more coming in late for practice. No more goofing off. I want you to have fun, but do that while you're playing, not instead of it."

Valerie turned around and scowled at Payton, but Neeka shot her a look back that made the girl instantly face forward.

"I'd like to invite Selina, Payton, and Neeka, your team leaders, to come down and speak now," Coach Gina said, waving them down. "As your teammates, I think they're the best choice to explain to you exactly the type of imprint you're making by playing for Hickory Academy."

I think I'm going to be sick, Payton thought as she walked over to stand next to Coach Gina.

Selina the Fearless stepped forward. "Listen, peeps, you've been given a role. It may not be a varsity one yet, but one day it will be. Your fellow varsity girls aren't gonna put up with your sour faces when the time comes. Better to learn to respect each other now than learn the hard way on varsity. Part of that is accepting the coaches' decision when it comes to who starts and who doesn't."

Watching the girls perk up as Selina spoke, Payton felt a wave of bravery wash over her. She cut in. "Varsity is going for its first undefeated season in the district. The only reason that is happening is because varsity is committed to every single drill and scrimmage at every practice. You don't earn the glory of being the best by gossiping when you should be practicing."

"Look at Payton," Neeka added. "Payton struggled at first, a lot. She wanted to be better, so she worked hard."

Payton look at the ground, embarrassed. She thought the whole point of this was to take the attention off her.

"Working hard is exactly that. It's not easy. But if volleyball were easy, everyone would be doing it. But they're not. Only a select few are, including you." Neeka pointed at the girls. "Payton understood that. So she perfected her jump serve. And now, she's one of the most important weapons the team has—both JV and varsity."

Payton looked up, straightening her posture, realizing just how far she had come. It was something she should be proud of, not embarrassed about.

Neeka continued. "So instead of blaming Payton for why you're not starting, look to her for inspiration. Find a role where you're needed most and perfect it. Or, at least, try to. Either way, you'll improve. And so will the team."

****

Instead of heading over to varsity practice, Coach Gina rang Coach Mike and explained that she needed to keep the girls at JV practice for a team bonding exercise. Payton watched as she held the phone out from her ear, no doubt to save her ears from whatever Coach Mike was screaming down the line.

When she hung up, her face broke out into a triumphant grin.

Looks like Coach Gina is well able to handle him, Payton thought.

The inflatable beach ball was put away for another day. Their coach wanted to get back to basics, as if they were starting fresh. As the team began a peppering drill to warm-up, some of the players tested Coach Gina on her newly asserted authority. Led by Val, they ignored her whistle to begin play, chatting away. But Coach Gina was quick to redirect them toward the bench, warning that next time it'd be an upcoming match they'd be sitting out.

Payton and Neeka looked at each other. Their expressions both screamed, "Did she really just do that!" Coach Gina had lived up to her word. Payton was delighted.

And it was effective. She watched as Val's expression turned from anger, then disappointment, before finally settling on one that resembled raw ambition—the same expression she carried around during the basketball season.

She's finally tapping into her inner athlete, Payton thought, relieved.

The tone for the rest of practice was very different. The girls made an extra effort to get along and to focus. They listened when others spoke. For the first time all season, JV started to feel like a real team, one where all the girls shared a common goal. Not to win, but to improve.

"You don't have to be great to start, but you do have to start to be great!" Neeka yelled happily during a passing drill.

But soon, Neeka's encouragement turned to something more Annette-like. "Your feet are out of position," she barked. "You can't pass with crooked feet!"

Payton was shocked. Neeka was taking her leadership role seriously, but maybe a little too much. Waving at her friend, she pushed her hands down, signally her not to be so intense.

After practice, Neeka thanked her for it. "Sorry, I got carried away," she confessed.

"I understand," Payton said. "It's easy to do."

"But at least we're making progress now!"

"I know! I'm so happy we decided to talk to Coach Gina again."

"Me too! I feel like we're headed in the right direction. And now we have proof that she's the one who wrote *Diary of a Young Volleyball Star.*"

"How?"

"In the book, the author has a really bad experience with a coach, to the point that she decides to write a letter to the local volleyball authority to make a formal complaint."

Payton bit her lip. "Bad coaches are everywhere. I'm sorry, jelly bean, but I still don't think she wrote it. I think we would know. She would have announced it, or our parents would have heard it through the grapevine. It's just too farfetched."

Neeka let it go, knowing there was no point debating it.

Payton quickly changed topics. "I am a little worried about what the freshmen think now. They probably feel like we squealed for revenge."

"Who cares?" Neeka said. "You can't please everyone. We did the right thing."

She was right. It didn't matter what the freshmen thought. The important thing was that JV was moving back on track.

CHAPTER 11

Dressed in bright red jerseys that reminded Neeka of strawberries, the Sycamore High School JV team sent a float serve their way, but it landed in the net.

The final point of the match went to Hickory Academy, who were in the lead by six.

"We won!" Janette yelled from the bench. "We actually won! That's twice now!"

The Sycamore girls looked absolutely disgusted. One even punched the net in frustration. It was not the ending they had expected.

"How did we lose to them?" one of their hitters spat. "They have the worst record in the district. This is so humiliating. We let them win on our home turf."

Her teammate patted her on the back. "No worries, we still have the tournament to play. They didn't even qualify. They're done and dusted for the season."

Neeka listened to them grimly. It was true what they said. Being the final week of district play, this was JV's last match of the season. They had won their last two matches, but it wasn't enough to qualify for the JV District Tournament. Still, it felt good to win. She'd been afraid varsity would finish the season undefeated while JV finished completely defeated. But thankfully, that hadn't happened. Varsity still had an unbeaten record, but JV now had a couple of wins under their belt as well.

At the sidelines, as the girls celebrated their victory, Neeka spotted Val sitting on a fold-up chair, away from everyone, looking slightly disturbed.

Neeka sat beside her. "Don't you prefer winning?" she joked, hoping to cheer the girl up.

Her comment hit a sore spot. Val smiled, but it was forced.

"What's wrong?" Neeka asked.

"You know, just that it's over. When I decided to join volleyball, I imagined being the star *libero* who took Hickory Academy all the way to the championships. I don't want the season to be over. I want to keep playing."

Actions have consequences. Her brother had predicted this—that the JV girls would one day be forced to look at their own behavior. If they hadn't spent the season goofing around, if they'd focused on the game rather than Payton, then there was a chance they would have been good enough to qualify for the JV District Tournament.

Val was an excellent *libero*. But talent only showed when put into action. More times than she should have been, she'd been more interested in goofing off than playing volleyball. If she'd performed well constantly throughout the season, Coach Mike might have added her to the varsity roster. Her own behavior had gotten in her way, a fact she was clearly realizing now.

Neeka hated the way the girls had treated Payton, but they were paying the price now. She wanted Val to learn from her mistakes, but she didn't want to shove them in her face.

"You know," she said softly, "my brother told me this might happen. You can really be a great player, but you have to show it to Coach Mike if you want to make varsity. My brother and I both agree that you definitely have what it takes to rock the court as *libero*. This season is over, but keep that in mind for next year. If you do, I'm sure you'll be wearing a varsity jersey."

This made Val feel better. Her eyes lit up, and she leaned in closer to Neeka to whisper, "Jamari really said that? He thinks I can be a great *libero?*"

"Sure. He's been at most of our matches. He's seen you play. My brother's a top athlete himself. He can see talent where it's at."

"OMG!" Val squealed. "Your brother is so hot!"

Neeka was afraid the girl might faint. "Okay, calm down. He's no Bruno Mars."

Val sat up straighter. "Hey, did varsity touch the lucky doorknob today?"

In the library of their school, there was a stained glass doorknob hanging on a back wall that had survived a fire that broke out in the building long ago. Originally an art project, it was believed to have saved an entire classroom full of students from being trapped in the flames of the fire. It currently hung on a marble plaque with the words "Even the most unassuming wonders guard these walls" engraved into it.

Though a majority of the student body had ignored the lucky doorknob for years prior, the volleyball team had each touched it last year. Seeing how well their last two seasons had been, and being unbeaten so far, the superstition was catching on. Before major games, more and more teams were starting to touch the glass case the doorknob was enshrined in.

"Of course we did!" Neeka said, answering Val's question. "I remember watching it sparkle blue, green, purple, and yellow last year, wondering if it truly was lucky. And here we are. About to close out the regular season undefeated. I'm pretty sure our success so far this season has mostly been due to hard work, not superstition, but you never know, do you?"

"I guess you'll know for sure tonight," Val determined. "Because if you lose against Sycamore, a team even we just beat, I would consider that very, very unlucky."

****

With the JV match behind them, Team Scary Pancake had their varsity match to think about. Varsity would be going on to play at the District Tournament, and that was already decided, so it wasn't goodbye. But they were going for an undefeated record. They hadn't lost a single match all season. They were at the top and wanted to stay there.

"Did you see a photographer is here?" one of the juniors asked as they filtered into the boys' locker room.

Neeka always thought meeting in the boys' locker room was the funniest part of playing an away game. The girls' locker rooms tended to smell much better, full of perfume and body spray. Didn't guys wear deodorant and cologne? You could never tell standing in one of their locker rooms.

"You're talking about photographers?" Coach Mike asked sharply. "You might as well call defeat and head home now. How the heck do photographers tie into volleyball? Please, someone answer me."

"They don't," the junior mumbled.

"Exactly. You got to keep your head in the game, girls. A quick show of hands. How many of you think we're going to crush the competition tonight?"

Everyone raised their hands.

"Wrong answer!" He threw down his clipboard. "This is volleyball, not a birthday party. There are no guarantees. Look at JV. Everyone assumed they would lose tonight, but they won. It was clear the Sycamore team had no respect for our JV girls at the start of the match. They were overconfident, and they paid for it. What have I been saying to you all week? Knox?"

"Don't take the last opportunity for granted," Lacey answered.

"Exactly. Don't automatically think you can beat them. Respect the effort they've put in to preparing for this match. That's the only way you will stay sharp."

"Yes, Coach," the girls said, allowing their egos to deflate.

"That doesn't mean I want you gals to give up your fight. We're trying to do something we've never done before—to finish the season undefeated. I understand it's not easy. But if you want to walk out of here tonight with a perfect regular season, don't presume anything. Work for it, like you have done."

****

Neeka didn't know if it was Coach Mike's speech or if Hickory Academy was simply more advanced, but by the middle of the second set, they were cruising through. Like seriously, the other team had only managed to score one point in the first set and had struggled to score four more so far in the second set. The Sycamore girls simply weren't skilled enough to handle Hickory Academy's attack.

During a time-out, Neeka looked up into the bleachers just in time to see her papa climbing up to the steps toward Jamari and her ma.

He made it! she sang inside.

Knowing how she felt, Jamari gave her a thumbs up.

Returning to the court, the second half of the set played out the same. The team got into an easy rhythm passing, setting, and spiking. They never lost their serve, but continued to score point after point. By the start of the third set, the fans looked bored. A small few were even clearing the bleachers.

Neeka was afraid it might be going a little too easy. Maybe this was part of their strategy—make Hickory Academy overconfident, then crush them by bringing out a secret weapon, like they did with Payton. She wanted to start feeling excited that they were actually going to pull off ending the regular season with an unbeaten record, just as some of her fellow varsity members were already doing, but she didn't want to lose focus. Coach Mike's words kept repeating in her head. The match wasn't over until the fat hillbilly sang. The other team could come back and beat them.

With the game going so well, Neeka had barely broken a sweat. She still had a lot of energy and hadn't needed Lacey to replace her as setter. She felt bad for it and wondered if she should fake an injury, though it went against everything she believed in. But this was the seniors' last regular season match—ever. The other seniors were in the starting line-up, so were already playing, but Lacey hadn't left the bench.

The guilt Neeka felt about starting over Lacey proved unnecessary. A few points into the third set, when it became more than apparent Hickory Academy would walk away victorious, Coach Mike informed the ref that he wanted to substitute two players. He called Neeka off the court and put Lacey in.

They met in the substitution zone near the scoring table, facing each other, and waited for an official to record their numbers.

"The last hurrah," Lacey said. "I can't believe this is my last regular season game. Enjoy every minute, Neeka, because it goes by way too fast."

Once their numbers were recorded, they quickly switched places.

As Lacey walked onto the floor, the crowd erupted into wild applause, standing on their feet to cheer Lacey on. "We love you, Lacey!" a few of the boys yelled. The cheerleaders waved their pompoms around while the other fans in the bleachers vigorously shook their banners.

Touched, Lacey placed her hand over her heart as she faced her supporters. Though no one could hear her over the cheers, she said, "Thank you so much, but all y'all better stop or I won't be able to set." Then, sniffling with bittersweet emotions, she took her place on the court.

From the sideline, Neeka wiped away her own tears. The seniors didn't have many game days left. After today, there were only the tournaments to play. She couldn't bare the idea of not having Lacey around next year. She didn't know what college Lacey was going to; Lacey didn't know herself yet whether it'd be local or far away, but Neeka hoped the senior found some time to visit them whenever she was home.

"God, not you too. Tough up, Leigh," Selina moaned, though she had a single black tear streak down her face, leaving smudged eyeliner.

Letting Lacey have her moment first, Coach Mike then subbed in Payton as a hitter. Neeka was surprised, so she could only imagine how

Payton felt. In the varsity matches, Payton was usually only subbed in to serve, not to stay on as hitter.

"Go Payton!" she screamed, delighted for her friend.

Payton beamed as she took her place.

"Should be me," Selina grumbled.

Neeka patted her on the knee. "Don't be jelly. You've gotten plenty of playing time on varsity this season."

The rest of the third set didn't take long. The rallies were short, the serves quick. Hickory Academy closed out the match 25-1, 25-4, 25-2.

They'd finished the season undefeated.

The uproar from the crowd was deafening. It was hard to believe they were at an away game. Hickory Academy totally dominated the gym. Celebrating with the team, their fellow classmates stampeded down onto the floor, hugging and cheering. They threw their banners into the air like graduation caps. It was a chaos. Sweet, victorious chaos.

From somewhere nearby, drops of some orange power drink hit Neeka's skin. Someone was splashing it all over the team.

Wow, she kept thinking. *This is... wow.*

There was no doubt now—Hickory Academy would be entering the District Tournament as the favorites to win.

No one was going home that night. The team, along with most of the school, gathered at a local diner to celebrate. As they sipped their colas and chewed their burgers and pizza slices, their classmates lined up to congratulate them, as did many of the diner's regulars, who didn't seem at all bothered that their meal had been invaded by a school-sized group of animated teens.

"This is kind of like last year," Lacey said loudly. It was becoming difficult to carry on a conversation over the noise.

"What do you mean?" Payton asked.

"Our season last year was so unexpected. No one thought we'd make it all the way to Sub-State. It was a place we never thought we'd be. And now, here we are—our first undefeated season so soon after. I wish I could play volleyball for Hickory Academy forever, but if this has to be my final year on the team, I'm glad it happened this way."

A thought suddenly occurred to Neeka. "Not to be a kill joy, but you know what this means... All the teams in the district are going to be gunning for us. At the tournament, we're going to be hunted down."

"I'm not worried," Lacey said confidently. "You can't stop a pack of wolves when they're hungry."

At home, Neeka shut out the lights and slid under her covers, looking at the thousands of glow-in-the-dark stars around her room. Not for the first time, she wondered if it was possible to play volleyball in space. Whenever she made it up in a rocket, she'd be sure to bring a volleyball with her and see.

She'd assumed she'd be exhausted after such a big day, but the adrenaline of victory was still pumping through her. It made it impossible to sleep. She turned on her reading lamp and pulled out *Diary of a Volleyball Star*. She was nearing the end of the book. The author, whoever she really was, was entering her final year playing for her college team.

I made captain today! Now that I'm a senior and the other girls have moved on, I am the best girl on the team. There's no harm in admitting that, right? Not to you, diary. My stats are some of the most admired in the nation. That's why they call me a star, though I'm not sure I like that term. I'd prefer they use the term "accomplished athlete" or something. But after our team won NCAA Women's Volleyball Championships last year, I was elevated to star status. I've been interviewed in a few magazines since then and even appeared on a daytime talk show! Already, I've been offered a few pro contracts, but I'm not signing anything yet.

Volleyball will always be a part of my life. A treasured part. But I feel other things in life pulling at me. I'd love a career as a marine biologist. It's what I've been studying during my time here, after all. I declared my major junior year... After Courtney... Anyway, I don't want to talk about that right now, diary. But I guess it makes sense why I chose Marine Biology. I want to help preserve life, to protect those who can't help themselves. Even if it is a simple starfish I'm helping, or a dolphin.

Also, I met a boy. I mean, I've met lots of boys in college, most of them bird brains, but this guy is so different. He's not as cute as most guys I'd go for, but he is really interesting. We talk for hours over Instant Messenger. He really makes me laugh! And he treats me so well. I'm not used to it, if I'm being honest. I met him at the afterschool program I've been volunteering at. He was a new tutor who started at the end of last year, so I helped him get his ropes. We then met up a few times during the summer. And now... Well, we're dating. And it just feels so right. We fight, all couples do, but there's no unnecessary drama. I dare say that this is the man I might marry. Wow. It feels so weird writing that. But it's true.

This is but another positive experience I've had volunteering at the afterschool program. I mean, the area is rough. Sometimes we get egged walking to the building. And when we play volleyball in the courtyard, there's a high metal fence to keep out the local teenagers at night. But it has so been worth it. I really enjoy the reward tutoring offers. I guess if Marine Biology doesn't work out, I can always be a teacher.

I've gotten off track, diary! Sorry! So much has happened since I last wrote in you. I'm out of practice. So Captain! I wasn't surprised when Coach told me I'd be leading the team this year, but it was still a great honor. Happy and sad at the same time. Senior year of college means one thing—my last year in this type of team environment. If I do decide to go pro, I know it will be nothing like this. I think being paid somehow diminishes the sport. I know it's necessary, I'm not denying that everyone has to make a living, but I like the purity of playing at a level where we feel fulfilled based on our passion alone.

I know it won't be easy. I was the captain of my high school team as well. When you're in a leadership role like that, you feel a lot of pressure. Every mistake the team makes, you feel it is your own. And you're constantly fluctuating between just being one of the girls and being the boss. It's a lot to take on. I hate it when I have to reprimand one of my teammates. I feel like that's Coach's job. But this is college-level volleyball. Coach isn't here to play babysitter. We're all adults. We have to work things out on our own. Sometimes, a team just needs a central figure to look toward for guidance. Right now, that's me.

Neeka stopped there, feeling her eyelids start to droop. She was learning so much from the book. There was a lesson in every entry the author wrote. Tonight's entry helped her to realize what a delicate balance it was being a team leader and a teammate as well. With JV, all of Team Scary Pancake had experienced the anxiety that can come from leading not only their teammates but their classmates as well. Sometimes, it meant standing up to them as much as it meant standing with them.

She was glad Coach Gina was so supportive. Granted, it'd taken the woman a bit of time to get there, at least where it concerned the team's attitude, but she could have just as easily dismissed the concerns of the girls. At least she'd taken the time to explain to them her own coaching philosophy and hadn't shut the door when they'd approached her a second time.

These days, Neeka wasn't entirely sure anymore if the author of the book was Coach Gina or not. Payton's doubt was starting to creep into her mind as well. Coach Gina was very private about her life away from the court. Neeka knew she was married, but she had no idea if she even had kids. Furthermore, she never talked much about her career in college. The only reason they knew she'd been a top athlete was because there was buzz when she was hired on as the assistant coach. But Coach Mike had been a top athlete himself. That didn't mean either of them were doing daytime talk shows at university.

I guess some things are just meant to remain a mystery, Neeka thought as she fell into a deep, dream-filled sleep.

CHAPTER 12

The atmosphere at varsity practice changed in the week leading up to the District Tournament. Before, while closing out the regular season, their focus had been on maintaining their undefeated record. That was over. Now, they wanted to conquer the championship tournaments. District. Regionals. Sub-State. And State.

Their preparation was entirely different. They couldn't worry about the potential of losing a match. They would be paired up against really strong teams, especially if they made it to Regionals and beyond. It was natural they might lose a match or two along the way. The important thing was that they stayed in the competition.

Last year at Sub-State, they had almost won. It'd been a very close match. Now, Hickory Academy was stronger than it ever had been. Their undefeated season was a testament to that. As she listened to Coach Mike lecture them about how volleyball was as much about observation as it was perspiration, Neeka knew they had a really good chance at making it to State this year.

But first, they had to get through the District Tournament.

Neeka assumed the District Tournament would be exhausting, but like their last match of the regular season, they breezed through it, all the way to the Final.

But as she stood on the court facing the Demonbreun High girls, she knew the Final wouldn't be so easy. These girls were ruthless. As the team who usually dominated the district until Hickory Academy had stolen the spotlight last year, Demonbreun High was known for coming back with a vengeance.

"You're going down," one of the girls in yellow and black whispered to her during the handshake, low enough that no officials could hear.

"Really, because from what I can remember, we already beat you once," Neeka retorted.

Having won the coin toss, their opponents earned the right to serve first. It was an ace, landing on Hickory Academy's side untouched.

Uh oh, we're in trouble. Neeka could almost see the eyes of the Demonbreun High girls glowing red. She tried to make her own eyes do the same.

"Don't let them get to you," Coach Mike yelled. "You've beaten them plenty of times before. You'll do it again!"

Demonbreun High scored again, but this time after a long rally.

While the ball continued being passed back and forth, Neeka noticed an unmistakable divide among the crowd. The bleachers were filled with teams, locals, parents, and fans from all over the district. It was odd what an undefeated season could do. Some of the crowd wanted Hickory Academy to push forward, tired of Demonbreun High's reign over the decade, but the other half clearly wanted Hickory Academy to lose, simply because they hadn't yet this season.

We're no longer the underdogs, that's for sure, Neeka mused. *I know everyone likes an underdog, and I knew the other teams would be out for blood, but I didn't think this many people would start hating us just because we were champions.* It was the exact opposite of what she thought would happen. Paired up with another school, yeah, maybe. But going against Demonbreun High—she thought they'd be perceived as heroes.

Shaking it away, she returned to the game. Hickory Academy had won the serve, but Demonbreun High returned it easily. Neeka positioned herself, waiting for her teammates to pass the ball to her. She set it for an outside hitter who slammed it across the net. But the

Demonbreun defense players dived to dig the ball and it eventually came flying back over. Realizing she was in a perfect position to tip it over the net, Neeka did so. It was unexpected, and Demonbreun High wasn't able to get to it in time.

"Nice dump!" Selina yelled from the sidelines.

The remainder of the match was equally erratic, with the main strategy on either side being to outsmart the other team. It was a match of wills as much as it was precision and timing. Demonbreun High were determined to destroy Hickory Academy. They battled it out into the fifth and final set.

It had been true for many matches, but today it was especially valid. Payton's jump serve saved the day. Coach Mike unleashed it halfway through the fifth set. It was enough to give Hickory Academy the advantage it needed to take home the District Tournament trophy.

As they took to the podium, the commentator announced what they were all thinking. "And Hickory Academy remains undefeated this season."

His words were gold.

****

The following morning was a Sunday—the one day of the week her parents let her sleep in. But Neeka had too much to do. Rather than lying in bed, she jumped out and dressed. Basketball season was starting soon. Team Scary Pancake was going to meet up at the mall and go shopping for new gear. Then they were going to practice at Payton's house.

The idea of basketball try-outs worried them all. They had played on JV together last year, but more than likely, this year, Payton would play for varsity while Neeka stayed on JV. Selina could go either way. Basketball wasn't like volleyball. The program was long established, and there was a lot of competition. There would be no going back and forth between teams like Team Scary Pancake did in volleyball.

It had been Payton's idea to practice. Mumbling something about the stars, she'd said it would be worth it in the end. Volleyball season was nearly over. As much as they needed to concentrate on the tournaments, they also had to look ahead to what was next. Basketball.

Payton's words had been convincing, but Neeka knew their extra practice probably wouldn't help change the inevitable. It was worth a try, though. She really didn't want to be stuck on JV alone. She felt bad thinking it, but she secretly hoped Selina stayed on JV with her.

Something smelled like bacon. Following her nose downstairs, she poked her head into the kitchen, surprised to find her papa there. She'd expected her family to still be sleeping, especially her papa, who often slept in because of his late nights at work.

"Good morning," Donald greeted his daughter, flipping the bacon in a pan. "There are some bagels there if you're hungry. The bacon will be done in a moment."

Neeka grabbed a bagel off the plate and smothered it in honey and butter. "Why you up so early?"

"I got a call from one of the nurses on the morning shift at work." He left the bacon to fry as reached across the counter to grab the morning's newspaper. Grinning as if he had a joke to tell, he handed her the newspaper. "Open it up to the sports section."

Doing as she was instructed, Neeka quickly flipped to the back of the paper. She saw headlines about the Titans and the upcoming season of the Predators, but she didn't see anything too exciting—

She gasped when she flipped to the next page. There was a write-up about Hickory Academy's undefeated volleyball season and their win in the District Tournament. "The New Queens of the Court" the headline read. Above the story, taking up half of the page, was a photo of her in her mostly blue jersey setting the ball.

"Oh my stars!" she screamed. "Is this for real!?"

"Well, it's not a ghost paper."

She couldn't believe it. It was completely surreal looking at herself in the paper. If it weren't for the strong smell of bacon, now burning as Donald looked adoringly at her, she would swear she was dreaming.

Jamari lazily joined them in the kitchen, his hair sticking in all directions. "Papa, you're up," he observed, just as surprised as Neeka had been. "I was having the best dream. Lacey and I were fighting alien warships together. Girl looked smoking in her tight uniform. Then a bunch of screaming woke me up. It better be good."

He reached for a bagel but Neeka stopped him, shoving the paper in his face. "It was. And stay away from my friend."

"Do you mean the bagel or Lacey?" he asked, but took the paper from her and studied the photo. "You blinked," he joked, though he hugged her proudly. "Good job, sis. We should frame it."

"Papa—the bacon," she said when one caught a small flame.

"Oh no!" He scrambled to remove the pan from the stove.

"Did Ma see this yet?" she asked.

"I was thinking we could bring her breakfast in bed and show her," her dad said. "Minus the bacon."

****

The shopping trip at the mall with the girls turned out to be a lot of fun. It was just the type of activity they needed to release the tensions they had about returning to Regionals to defend their title. There weren't a lot of stores in the mall. It was pretty small compared to others around Nashville. But it was close to their school, where they had their parents drop them off before walking the rest of the way.

"I think we might have to get a taxi back to the school," Payton said under the mass of bags she was carrying.

For a girl who claimed to be a diehard tomboy, she sure liked to shop. By the time they left the sporting store, Payton had a gazillion bags under her arms.

"Well, you're definitely one of their favorite customers," Neeka laughed, helping her with some of the bags.

Selina didn't bother. "You bought it, you carry it," she said.

Looking at Payton's new collection, Neeka couldn't help but compare it to her one dinky bag. She didn't have the same allowance

Payton did. Her ma had given her a few extra twenties to cover the cost of new sneakers, the hard type they were required to wear during basketball games, but there'd been a lot more in the store she would have bought, if she could have.

Money can't buy love, but it sure can buy a lot of goodies, she sighed inwardly.

"So my mom said she wants me to get a job in the next few years," Payton said. "I have a hard enough time keeping up with my grades as it is. I don't get it. But Mom insists it would teach me financial responsibility and would look good on my college applications."

This piqued Neeka's interest. "I'll have to get a job soon too!" she said, almost excitedly. "Do you know what this means?"

"That neither of you will have any hope at a social life," Selina remarked.

"What?" Payton asked.

Neeka couldn't believe she didn't get it. "We can find a job together! There are so many possibilities, Payton. We don't have to get something boring like a fast food restaurant. We can work at the zoo, or at the bowling alley. Somewhere fun."

"I'm not sure it's legal to put job and fun in the same sentence together."

Neeka grinned. "Not even if we got jobs selling hot dogs at Titan football games?"

She couldn't see Payton's face clearly under all the bags, but she knew she'd won her friend over. "Maybe my mom is on to something," she said. "I'd tell her so, but then she'd never let me hear the end of it."

Suddenly, Payton tripped, and her bags went flying to the floor. Giving in, Selina helped her pick them up. "I think you're right about that taxi," she said. "But let's ask it to stop at the smoothie place on the way."

"I prefer ice cream," Payton said. "Isn't there a milkshake stand around here somewhere?"

"But smoothies are so much healthier," Selina objected. "Remember, we have Regionals in only a week."

Payton continued her search for the milkshake stand. "Then I'll get mine with strawberries."

****

The Regional Tournament arrived. It was nothing like the District Tournament. The venue was bigger. The media was bigger. And the competition was bigger. Here, at Regionals, a topspin jump serve was nothing new. Almost every team had someone who could serve just as well as Payton could. Maybe even better. Time would tell.

As reigning champions, the girls were prepared for the fight. They didn't let the enormous stadium of the university that hosted the event get to them. Or the flashing lights coming from the press box. Their eyes were on one thing—the trophy. Not just so they could keep their crown, but because it was a bridge to State. Technically, they didn't have to win. The top two teams at Regionals moved forward onto Sub-State. But winning meant they were more likely to have a home court advantage at the Sub-State match.

Having been featured in the local media because of their undefeated season, they were treated like mini celebrities. At one point, a little girl heading toward the bleachers pointed at Neeka and shouted, "There's the girl from the paper!" Neeka didn't know how to handle it, wondering what the author of *Diary of a Young Volleyball Star* would do.

She would stay focused on the game, Neeka told herself. *There's no cruising through this tournament.*

As the bleachers filled at the start of their first match, Neeka realized just how right she was. They were paired against Vanderbilt High School, a sprightly team with mediocre skills. This was the first time in years Vanderbilt had qualified for Regionals. Hickory Academy was much more skilled and experienced, so it should have been an easy win, yet they struggled from the start. Despite all the media hype around them, Neeka and her teammates somehow managed to maintain their concentration, but it wasn't enough to keep them at the top of their game. They didn't perform terribly, but their coordination was slightly off, preventing them from scoring points they should have.

"Let's turn the heat up!" Neeka shouted midway through the match.

"Undefeated until the end!" Selina added.

Coach Mike wasn't so optimistic. "Don't let the pressure of the tournament get to you!" he bellowed from the sidelines. "You're tensing up! Work through those nerves!"

By the fifth set, things looked hopeful. Hickory Academy was gaining on Vanderbilt's lead. Neeka thought there was time to catch up, to prove they were the stronger team, but the damage had been done. Vanderbilt had gone into the match assuming they would lose. Their surprising performance, even after they lost the third and fourth set, gave them the confidence they needed to push hard, all the way until the end.

Vanderbilt won.

Hickory Academy lost, ending their perfect run.

It was hard to swallow. The attention surrounding them at Regionals made their defeat all the more bitter. It wouldn't be pushed away quietly, like it had been for the other teams who had lost their first match. It would be whispered from one fan to the next that Hickory Academy had lost to Vanderbilt High School, a lesser team.

"I can't believe it," Selina whined, her shoulders slumping against the chair in the classroom that had been designated as their changing room during the tournament. "We're no longer undefeated."

"We knew it couldn't last." Lacey tried to console her.

"But did you hear the way the crowd cheered when we lost?" Selina protested. "They were happy the other team broke our perfect record. It was insane."

Lacey affectionately smoothed down Selina's hair. "That just shows how far we've come. You know you've made it when you have both lovers and haters in the stands."

A knock on the door of the classroom interrupted them. "Y'all decent?" Coach Mike asked from the other side.

Selina rolled her eyes, her mood unwavering. "Great, now a lecture."

"Don't let him hear you say that," Neeka scolded her as Lacey invited Coach Mike to come in.

He took a seat on top of one of the desks. He was a tall, athletic man. Neeka feared the desk would collapse underneath him. It certainly looked as though it had shrunk under his weight.

"I know you're all disappointed we lost, but you need to look at how long we survived before losing. Celebrate that instead." The softness in his face instantly disappeared. "And stay focused! We still have the rest of today and tomorrow to get through. So any tears over losing stop now. Our next match is in less than an hour. Stay warm. Hydrate up. And don't lose focus on what's to come. We're not giving up our trophy that easily!"

Selina smiled, her mood lifting.

Next to her, a junior shouted, "Holla players!" It was funny coming from the petite mousy girl.

"Good," Coach Mike said. "That's the spirit. No matter what happens, carry that energy with you all the way to the end."

With one match already lost, Neeka hoped the end didn't come too soon.

****

Hickory Academy fought through. They'd nearly lost their second match as well, their confidence knocked, but Coach Mike had pulled out the newspaper from the previous Sunday, reminding them of their own power and talent to succeed. It was a bold but rewarding move. They got it together in time to win the second match. And the next. And then again.

No one escaped the Regional Tournament undefeated. The teams were too closely matched in their skill level. By the afternoon of the last day, many teams had lost more than the one match Hickory Academy had. It put Hickory Academy in the Semi-Finals.

And, in the end, the Final.

They were playing the River Rats. Neeka couldn't believe that was their official mascot, but it was. The girls had also been undefeated in their district, only to lose a match at Regionals. Going in, Hickory Academy knew it would be the biggest of their battles so far this year. There was a good chance they might not survive it.

The first set was telling. They battled tooth and nail. Their hitters were incredible, some of the best Neeka had ever played against. Ball after relentless ball was pounded toward their side. It was hard to keep up, but Hickory Academy did, enough to keep the score close. But the River Rats were that much better and took home the set.

Taking her position in the right back corner of the court to prepare for the second set, Neeka watched as her own team went silent, entirely focused on their opposition. Their energy changed. They wanted this win. Victory was the only option. The River Rats may be excellent hitters, but now, Hickory Academy would be a steel wall. No. Titanium.

When the serve was made, Neeka ran from the back row to her setting position near the front. Having started in the back, she wasn't allowed to attack the ball, not that she normally would anyway, but she could block, given the opportunity to.

She didn't need to. Selina was on it, her arms stretched tall near the net, but careful not to touch it. Blocked by Selina, the ball never made it to their side, a pattern that repeated itself throughout the remainder of the set.

Titanium.

The River Rats were disoriented. It was clear they relied heavily on their spikes. With their offense down, they were forced to dig the ball—not their strong point. The game slowed down; they were no longer able to bombard Hickory Academy like they had in the first set.

"Where did this team come from?" she heard a girl on the other side of the court ask out loud.

By the fifth set, they were all exhausted. The game had dragged on a lot longer than either side expected. But the River Rats didn't have one thing. They didn't have Payton. Yes, a few of them could perform a jump serve, but none like Payton could. If Regionals was proving anything, it was that Payton really was a master when it came to the serve.

As soon as Coach Mike subbed in Payton, Neeka knew Hickory Academy was going to be Regional Champions once more.

And they were.

The girls accepted their trophy then posed for a team photo. They were ecstatic. By making it to the Final, they already had the joy of knowing they would move on to the Sub-State Tournament, but defending their championship title by winning made it all the sweeter. It was a poignant moment for many of the girls, especially the seniors. Having lost at Sub-State last year, Neeka knew many of them believed this would be the last trophy they brought home.

But Neeka wasn't satisfied with Regionals alone. It wasn't enough for her. For the last two seasons, the one thing Hickory Academy had done well was surprise people, to excel beyond other's expectations. There was no reason that should change.

She wanted to win State.

Team Scary Pancake had made a vow that this would be their year to go all the way. So though Neeka held the Regionals trophy in her hand, she wouldn't be happy until it was replaced with the one they brought home from State.

CHAPTER 13

Sudden death.

It was an appropriate name for a knock-out round. Technically, that's what Sub-State was—a knock-out round to determine who played at State. But to Neeka, it was so much more. If they lost, like they had at Sub-State last year, it would mean the death of their season, the death of having Lacey as a teammate, and the death of their dreams to go to State.

Neeka wanted victory so badly. They only had one match to prove themselves worthy to play at the top. This was it.

Yes, it was sudden death, but the morning was going agonizingly slowly as they waited to play that afternoon.

At least they had the venue on their side. They were hosting their Sub-State match at Hickory Academy. It meant louder fans. Familiarity with the court. And the comfort of being at home. Statistically, teams did better when they had the home court advantage. That's why it was an advantage.

But none of it changed the fact that they were playing against Cumberland Lake High School. Not that Cumberland Lake had a huge reputation around the state. Hickory Academy was still confident they could win, even though they were trying not to let it show, knowing they had to stay grounded. Little was known about Cumberland Lake, except that they had come second in their Regionals, qualifying only because the first and second place teams got to advance forward. That was hopeful.

But one thing Cumberland Lake did have, the thing that made the Hickory Academy girls nervous, was a solid group of jump servers. Coach Mike had already warned them of this. Their servers were good, better than any they'd seen at Regionals. It meant Hickory Academy couldn't rely on Payton as a secret weapon. If they wanted to win, varsity would have to be fundamentally sound. In practice that week, they'd all worked hard to round out their skills.

Still, even with a team full of wicked servers, Cumberland Lake came in second at their Regionals, and we came in first. That's got to say something, Neeka thought as she hurried to class after hearing the warning bell for third period.

Why couldn't it be the end of the day? She just wanted to play, but the day refused to go by any faster.

So slow.

The nervous excitement around the school didn't help. Everyone was certain they'd go on to win State. They'd had an undefeated regular season, and they'd played at Sub-State before, so they were experienced. It sounded like a winning formula.

Stay grounded, she reminded herself for the hundredth time.

"You girls should wear those every day!" a guy said as Neeka scurried past him down the hall.

"Gross!" she shouted back. "Our uniforms are not for your viewing pleasure!"

Varsity was dressed up for the big day. The school administration had given them permission to wear their uniforms that day, including their short shorts and jerseys. Many of the girls, including herself, had also added a bit of make-up to their faces. Actually, everyone had, except Payton.

"Athletes don't wear make-up," Payton had said in disgust.

"Yes, they do," Neeka insisted. "Look at Gabby Douglas, the famous teen gymnast. Or even the WNBA. All the big sports celebrities wear it for press shoots, professional photos, posters... Not all female athletes are tomboys. Some are quite glam."

"Not this one," Payton said, sticking out her tongue.

It wasn't just the varsity girls who had made an effort. The student body had worked around the restriction of their uniforms, putting streaks of glitter in their hair and painting their faces blue and green— Hickory Academy's colors. The band had even replaced their shoelaces with blue florescent ones.

Making it to third period just as the clock changed the hour, Neeka flopped into the desk next to Payton. They shared History together—a subject that fascinated Payton but left Neeka counting the tiles on the walls.

Without saying a word, Payton pointed toward the whiteboard. On the top in blue marker read:

Watch varsity volleyball make History tonight at Sub-State. Good luck girls!

"I guess history is repeating itself," Payton joked. "They did the same thing last year."

"Yeah, I remember," Neeka said.

"Are you starting to feel the pressure?" Payton whispered, though class hadn't started yet. "Because I sure am. I keep getting stopped in the hallway by classmates and teachers wishing me good luck."

"They mean well," Neeka defended, liking the message on the whiteboard.

"I know, but I can't concentrate in class. I can't do anything but think about our match later."

"Me neither," Neeka admitted. "I just want to play."

Payton sat back. "It is great, though, isn't it? All the support we're receiving. I remember the start of the season last year when only half the bleachers were filled. Now look at us. I'm trying to appreciate the effort everyone is making, even if I am about to pass out with nerves."

"You're a top athlete, Payton. You've literally played in national tennis matches and All-Star basketball games. Aren't you used to the pressure by now?"

"Those are things I'm good at. Volleyball is different. I know I've improved, but sometimes I still feel like a jellyfish on land. And you heard Coach Mike. My jump serve means nothing in this match."

"Doesn't that take the pressure off?" Neeka reckoned.

"No. It means this match is just going to highlight to Coach Mike how useless I am in every other way."

Today, of all days, was not the day for Payton to start getting insecure about her role on the team. She couldn't ride the wave of her jump serve forever. Maybe tonight would finally teach her that, so she didn't get so antsy when other people practiced the same serve. But Neeka bit her tongue. She didn't want to make Payton's nerves worse.

"Just keep reminding yourself that Cumberland Lake only came second in their Regionals," Neeka encouraged.

It didn't improve things for Payton. "Trust me, that doesn't mean a thing. Not at Sub-State."

****

After class, Neeka followed Payton to her locker. Along the way, students continued to shout out their support. Some even threw blue and green confetti at them.

"Mind if I stash my history book in your locker?" Neeka asked, already knowing Payton's combination by heart. Depending on where their classes were, they often used each other's lockers for various reasons throughout the day.

"Probably a good idea. Otherwise, we'll never make it to the cafeteria for lunch. Not the way we keep getting stopped. I feel like a tractor in a sand hole."

When they arrived at Payton's locker, Neeka burst out laughing. She couldn't help herself. Cut-out hearts that resembled basketballs were taped to the door, each one spelling out a letter in Payton's name. In the center was a real white rose. It stood out against the dark blue paint of the locker.

"Looks like you have a not-so-secret admirer," Neeka said between giggles.

"George," Payton sighed, almost with regret.

Neeka elbowed her in the side. "Quick, fake a smile. You know he's watching from somewhere. No reason to hurt his feelings, not after all this effort."

Payton put on an enormous smile, like the type politicians used. "I wish he'd accept that I just want to be friends," she said between her teeth.

"I don't think that boy will ever give up on you." Neeka shook her head. "He's love-struck."

"I wonder why he chose basketballs instead of volleyballs. He does know what today is, doesn't he?"

"Maybe he knows you better than you think he does. Maybe he wanted to show his support but without the added pressure."

A real smile took over Payton's fake one. "That's actually kind of sweet." Then she turned serious. "Hey, let's not talk about the match over lunch. We'll just psyche ourselves out. Is that okay?"

"Agreed," Neeka confirmed, knowing that even though they wouldn't talk about it, the match would be the only thing on their minds.

****

This was it. Match time. If they won, they would move on to State. If they lost... Neeka shook her head. Now was not the time to think about that. Now was the time to fight. That was the only way to ensure history didn't repeat itself.

Amid a gymnasium that was so packed, security actually had to turn students away due to fire and safety regulations, Hickory Academy scored the first point of the match.

Neeka breathed a sigh of relief. It had been a long rally. It was probably the toughest point they had earned all season. The Cumberland Lake girls were good, very good. But that first point proved one thing—Hickory Academy could beat them. They had a chance at State. All they had to do was score more points like it.

After three more points were scored, Neeka felt herself relaxing even more. They could do this. They could really, really do this. Shutting out her emotions, she didn't want to get too excited. She tried to clear away everything but what was happening in the immediate moment.

In the middle of a rally, a junior in the back row passed the ball toward her. She set it, responding to a hitter in the front row who had called the ball. Her serve was good, but the hitter's aim was off, and the ball was easily reached by a Cumberland Lake hitter, who pounded it back over the net, scoring their first point of the match.

We're still in the lead, Neeka told herself. *We just have to keep that lead.*

It was easier said than done. For the first time that afternoon, Hickory Academy got a taste of what Coach Mike had warned them about all week. The server tossed the ball in the air, jumped high, and pounded it toward Hickory Academy. With the ball spinning at what seemed like a thousand miles per hour, the back row couldn't dig it properly. It bounced off her teammate's arms and went out of bounds.

Point Cumberland Lake.

With their jump serves, Cumberland Lake continued to score. It was like being hit with target-seeking torpedoes. At one point, Neeka had to duck to avoid being hit in the face. She swore that was a violation. Coach Mike thought so too. He started screaming from the sidelines when the ref did nothing, but then walked it off after Coach Gina whispered in his ear, probably reminding him that the last thing they wanted to do was get on the ref's bad side with insults.

Hickory Academy had never dealt with this level of talent before. Even Payton's jump serve at practice, by far the best in their region, couldn't have prepared them for this type of attack. It was harsh.

Neeka refused to lose hope. She threw all her attention onto the ball, studying it like it was a meteor in the sky. *All is not lost. When we get the serve back, we'll just have to make sure we keep it. We've already shown we can score when we serve.*

Eventually, one of Cumberland Lake's serves went slightly out of bounds. They had gained a good lead over Hickory Academy, but this was only the first set. Even if Hickory Academy lost the set, the match was far from over. They'd lost first sets before and gone on to win the match.

"Now we know what to expect!" one of the seniors on her team shouted. "Just stay on them!"

Nodding her head, Neeka got into ready mode, her knees bent, ready to sprint into her setting position as soon as the ball was served.

The rally went on for ages, but Hickory Academy managed to score again. Neeka was surprised they had. She didn't like criticizing her own team, but they'd been messy. Scared, even. It was like David versus Goliath, but then David freezing in place the second Goliath moved forward.

Coach Mike called a time-out.

"You're losing your cool. So they have a powerful serve. Get over it. Just keep the ball in play, and you'll be fine. Watch Cumberland Lake as they serve. Pay attention to their body language. It'll help you calculate where they're going to serve next. Dig harder! Stick together! If someone calls the ball, be on guard to assist your teammate if things go bad. You've got this, girls!"

When Cumberland Lake won back the serve, Hickory Academy tried hard to follow Coach Mike's advice, but it was proving impossible. They couldn't dig the serves. The serves Cumberland Lake were sending were like lightning, leaving a roar throughout the gymnasium when they struck the ground.

Neeka's heart flew when they Hickory Academy *libero* finally got to one of the serves, but the pass to her was nearly a shank, a rogue pass that was unplayable. Neeka had to chase the ball down, causing her to set awkwardly to her hitters. The ball made it over the net, but Cumberland Lake were ready for it, blocking with very little effort.

It didn't get any better. Over the next half hour, Hickory Academy experienced a thorough beat down. Cumberland Lake played like college girls. Pros, even. Their spiking was precise. Their blocks high. And their serves killer.

Sudden death.

The term had a whole new meaning. There was nothing Hickory Academy could do. They were out-matched. Cumberland Lake had skills they simply didn't possess. Before the match was over, Neeka tried to come to terms with their impending loss, but when the ref called the match at the end of the third set, she couldn't help the disappointment that overwhelmed her.

The season was over. Hickory Academy was out. Cumberland Lake would be moving onto State.

****

Little was said in the locker room as the Hickory Academy girls processed their defeat. They took longer than normal to change, knowing this would be the last time to do so. The seniors were especially slow. Once they took their jerseys off, they were off for good.

Neeka couldn't bare the silence, so she left the locker room before any of the others. Compared to last year, she was handling the defeat quite well. She'd done her best. There was nothing she could have done differently. But she still felt like crying. The way the JV behaved this year, who knew if they'd be able to fill the shoes of the seniors? This may have been Hickory Academy's last shot at State.

As she walked back out into the gym wearing jeans and a tank top, her bag dragging miserably behind her, she was surprised to see half the student body had stuck around, waiting. With the gym to themselves after the Cumberland Lake fans had left to go celebrate, the Hickory Academy students clapped like maniacs and threw blue streamers made of crepe paper over her head. Rolls of it.

Blushing, Neeka suddenly wished she'd waited for Payton instead of walking out alone.

"That was unexpected," she said as she found Jamari in the crowd.

"We've been waiting for ages. What's taking you guys so long?"

"You'll know when you play your very last high school basketball game."

Jamari nodded, understanding.

The crowd cheered again as more of the volleyball team walked out. This time, Payton and Selina were among them.

"This is outrageous!" Payton exclaimed, taking a spot in the crowd next to her and Jamari. She waved to her parents standing just behind them.

"Couldn't you hear us cheer when Neeka came out?" Jamari asked.

"We just assumed something funny had happened. We didn't expect this."

Another group came out, mostly juniors.

That left just the seniors.

"Okay, this is the big one," Neeka shouted. The rest of the varsity girls lined up in front of the crowd, collecting scraps of blue streamers from the ground to throw.

Lacey was in mid-conversation with the rest of the seniors when they walked out. They stopped short when they saw the crowd, their mouths nearly dropping to the floor.

The cheerleaders started a chant. "Hip hip!"

"Hooray!" the crowd yelled.

There were meant to be a few more hip hips, but the streamers starting flying early, causing everyone to immediately clap and cheer.

"Well done on a great season!" someone yelled.

"You may not be going to State, but you still were undefeated during the regular season. No one can take that away," another said.

"You've done us all so proud!" That was Coach Gina, who was jumping up and down more enthusiastically than the cheerleaders and pep band combined.

Without knowing what else to do, the senior girls bowed, giggling madly as they did.

The rest of the varsity girls ran up to them and huddled together.

"You know, there's absolutely nothing we could have done differently," Lacey reassured them. "They were the better team. But this was the best season Hickory Academy volleyball has ever seen. We made history this year. Teams in the future will look to us for inspiration. Let's not forget that."

"Now we know how all the teams we squashed this year feel," Selina joked.

"I'll miss you gals," Lacey said. She was speaking to the team, but she looked specifically at Neeka, Payton, and Selina. "V-ball love forever."

"V-ball love forever," the team echoed then broke away for the very last time as a team.

* * * * * * * * * * * * * * * * * * * *

After the masses began to clear, Neeka pulled Payton aside. Her parents were waiting for her in the car, so she had to speak fast. She needed to say something important, but she hoped it didn't upset Payton too much.

"Lacey was right," Neeka said. "There's nothing we could have done differently. The trouble is, Cumberland Lake isn't even the best of the best. They came second in their Regionals. That means there are teams out there better than them."

"I know," Payton said. She sounded as if she knew where the conversation was heading. "Our entire team needs new skills. We'll never be able to compete at State otherwise."

"I'm glad you understand," Neeka said, "because you have to get over this jump serve obsession. Everyone on the team needs to learn how to do one, even me. Our weakness is that we're not well-rounded players, not like the players of Cumberland Lake were. We need to pump up our skills big time."

Payton adjusted her bag over her shoulder. "My dad is waiting for me. I better go."

Neeka stopped her. "Payton, are you listening to me?"

"Yes!" Payton exclaimed, though she didn't sound mad. "I get it. And I'm coming to terms with it, okay? But you have to realize, it means my role on the team is no longer unique. That puts me in danger of not making varsity next year. So just give me time to adjust, okay?"

Neeka knew it troubled Payton, but she needed to clarify. "Payton, you're missing the point. What I'm trying to say is none of our skills can be unique anymore. I'm not just talking about your jump serve. I'm talking about everything. We need to hit better, pass better. The whole hot dog stand."

Payton smiled, relaxing. "I always did like hot dogs."

CHAPTER 14

Under the city lights of the downtown area of Nashville, everything glowed, except for Payton's mood. Enjoying the cool breeze after the stuffy gymnasium, her dad had suggested they take a walk, leaving his car at the school. It was only fifteen minutes before they were standing under the shadows cast by the low-rise, dusty brick buildings of the historical center.

"Where should we eat?" he asked her.

Payton felt her stomach tighten. "I'm really not hungry."

Brandon ran a hand through his greying hair. "Okay, pumpkin. How about we just keep walking then. You might feel hungry soon."

It'd been an emotionally exhausting day, full of extreme highs and extreme lows. She hadn't been crushed by their defeat, but it did make her sad. Hickory Academy was a good team, but not as good as any of them had thought. There were districts surrounding them that emphasized volleyball a lot more. Due to their success the last two seasons, she had never realized before that out there in the great wide yonder were teams that made Hickory Academy look like turkeys.

Her dad bent down, picking a coin up off the ground. "A penny for your thoughts?"

"Next to those girls tonight, we looked like nothing more than a small private school with a new volleyball program."

"That's exactly what you are," he pointed out.

Payton disagreed. "No. We're something greater. We have so much potential. We won't be defined by how new we are or how small our school is."

Brandon put his arm around his daughter, pulling her close. "Wise words, mini me. Your father raised you well."

"You can't take all the credit."

"Nor would I. Your mom is doing a fantastic job too. I know you two don't always see eye to eye when it comes to your passion for sports, but it isn't easy for her either."

Not wanting to get into a parent talk, Payton quickly redirected the subject. "Focus, Dad. We're talking volleyball. The way Cumberland Lake played, it felt as though they were one of those ginormous schools on the 5A level. If that's the type of team we're going to meet every year, I don't think we'll ever advance to State."

Brandon stopped walking. "Payton, what's the first thing I taught you about sports?"

She smirked, despite her mood. "To always keep my eye on the ball."

"After that," he groaned.

"To never say never."

"Precisely. You have an entire year to prepare for next season. The team can accomplish a lot in a year."

"But not a miracle."

"You don't need a miracle," Brandon maintained. "You need extra help."

Payton wasn't comforted. "And where are we going to get that? It's not like the school can magically afford to hire pro instructors." She thought about it. "Actually, they are building a new music center... Can they afford to hire pro instructors?"

"No," Brandon said, cutting her off before she got too excited. "That project was funded by a huge mega country star who makes more money a second than I do in a month. We're privileged, but not that privileged."

"Then it's useless," Payton said.

Brandon guided her forward, continuing their walk. "Buck up.

140

Stranger things have happened. Now come on, I know you're hungry. Your stomach is talking louder than you are. Let's find something to eat."

****

A little over two months went by before the extra help they needed came to them—in the form of an idea.

Hickory Academy had recently returned from its holiday break, and basketball season was well underway. Payton had made varsity, as expected, and so had Selina. Neeka was on JV again, despite the extra practice they had put in prior to try-outs. For the first time since they started playing basketball together at the Y in fifth grade, they were separated.

Payton missed seeing her friend at practice, a sentiment she shared with her dad when he called her from Cincinnati.

"How's my super star?" he asked. "I heard Hickory Academy are doing pretty good, now that they have my daughter on their team."

"We're slamming it," Payton informed him happily. "It's such a relief to be doing something I'm good at again, but I have to admit, I miss volleyball. Mostly because of Neeka. We hardly see each other anymore."

She grabbed a red Twizzler from the jar on top of her desk. Her mom usually didn't let her keep snack food around, especially not in her bedroom, but the jar had been a present for her birthday, so her mom hadn't forbidden it, though she had tried on more than one occasion to casually replace the jar with a bowl full of mixed fruits and nuts.

"Volleyball camp," her dad said out of the blue.

That was bizarre. He made no sense. Payton chewed on her Twizzler, waiting for him to say more, but he didn't. "And..."

"That's the extra help you need for next season. It came to me out of nowhere when I was going over some building reports."

Her dad seemed pretty excited. It was odd.

"We already go to volleyball camp. It's at the community center, remember?"

"That's my point. The volleyball camp at the community center is fine, but it's not great. Elite champions go to the best training facilities money can buy. You need something bigger and better."

"But I like the camp we go to. The instructors there are really nice."

Brandon huffed into the phone. "Nice doesn't win State, Payton."

He had her there. "What are you suggesting?"

"Find a camp that works with much stronger teams. Get the same training Cumberland Lake High School is likely getting. Take it to a whole new level."

Payton was intrigued. "Are there camps like that around here?"

"Close enough. Some major volleyball camps are held by universities in the general area."

Now Payton was excited. "Can you go online and search with me, or are you still at work?"

"It's way past closing hour, but yes, I'm still at work. But I have some time to spare for my champ."

A few minutes later, after Payton had turned on her laptop, she received a message from her dad with a link inside. She quickly clicked on it. The camp looked good, but there was one major problem.

"Veto," she said. "It interferes with basketball camp."

After a brief search, she sent her dad a link, hopeful.

"Veto," he declared. "Payton, that's all the way in Texas!"

"But it's one of the best in the nation! And it's so pretty," she said longingly, referring to the bright gymnasium and stadium-style seats.

"Next," her dad insisted. "Let's keep it closer to home. Nowhere that requires an airplane. Or a train, for that matter."

"You can drive to Texas," she mumbled.

Through the phone, she heard her dad typing away. No harm letting him do the hard work, she thought, abandoning her post. Grabbing another Twizzler, she leaned back in her chair, staring at the ceiling, imagining what it would be like to play in a high-tech gymnasium like the one at the camp in Texas. She hoped she'd find out someday.

"Check your message. I think I found the perfect camp," her dad said, clearly pleased with himself.

Payton checked. It looked pretty decent. It wasn't as nice as the one in Texas, but it looked much more professional than the one at the community center. The university was relatively close, and some really good coaches taught there, including a woman who had been on the USA Olympic team a decade or so ago. And the dates worked out perfect.

"Bingo," she said. "This is the one."

****

Discussing volleyball camp with her dad helped Payton realize something. She wouldn't always hold a special role on the team. She was learning to accept that. But she could still be an asset, a leader, by being proactive about the future of the Hickory Academy volleyball program, just like Lacey had explained to them months before.

The previous day, an important package had arrived. After their conversation on the phone, her dad had requested that the university hosting the volleyball camp send a few brochures and other useful information to Payton's address. She now held the material in her hand as she walked up the stairs to Coach Mike's office during lunch.

The door was wide open when she reached it. Coach Mike was bent over his desk, scribbling away at a notepad. A large bowl of popcorn sat untouched next to him.

Wow. Coach Mike not eating. I hope he's okay, she thought.

"Coach?" She announced her presence, knocking gently on the door.

He leaned back when he saw her. "You don't look like one of my creative writing students," he teased.

"I didn't know you taught creative writing," Payton said.

143

"I'm a man of many talents, Moore." He spread his hands out wide. "So tell me, what brings you here? Got lost in a time warp and thought it was volleyball season?"

Payton placed the volleyball camp material on his desk in front of him. "This."

"Brochures?"

"Volleyball camp brochures. If we want to be elite champions, we have to train like them."

"Those your dad's words?" he assumed.

"Yep," Payton said proudly.

He casually picked up one of the brochures. "Yeah, that sounds like Brandon. Good guy, your dad. I'm glad I've gotten a chance to know him this year. He misses you like crazy, you know."

Payton nodded, not sure how to respond.

He took a few minutes to flip through the information. At times, he grunted, but with Coach Mike, that could mean anything. When he finally put the material down, he looked at her, impressed. "I think it's a great idea."

Payton smiled, excited, but he raised a finger.

Uh oh. A finger raise was never good.

"But I can't be the one to make the final decision. It has to be a team vote. If you can get Coach Gina and the rest of the girls on board, JV and varsity, I'm in. For now, you have my blessing to ask them."

"Great!" Payton said, gathering up the material. "I know I can convince them."

She was about to leave, but Coach Mike called her back.

"Good initiative, Moore," he said with approval. "You're just what varsity needs."

On her way back from Coach Mike's office, Payton ran into Selina.

"Good news!" she chirped.

"Now that you're sixteen and old enough to date, you and George are finally a couple?" Selina guessed.

Was she crazy? "No! I haven't talked to him in weeks. We're just

144

friends. This is way more exciting." She held up a brochure for Selina to see.

"What, you going off to college early or something?"

Payton shoved it closer to Selina's face. "It's not a university brochure. It's for volleyball camp! A really good volleyball camp. One teams like Cumberland Lake go to."

Catching on, Selina grabbed the brochure from her, studying it carefully, her smile growing by the second.

"Keep it. They sent a few. What do you think?"

Selina was clearly tickled. "Payton, this is a rock'n idea. How'd you come up with it?"

"My dad helped me."

Selina tucked the brochure into her backpack. "Thank God for moms and dads with some athletic background. Does Coach know?"

Payton jumped up and down. "I just came from his office. He's totally in. We just have to convince Coach Gina and the rest of the girls, and then it's all settled!"

Selina grabbed her arm. "I saw Neeka down by the library reading that book she's always carrying around. Let's go tell her the good news."

Trying to keep quiet when they entered the library and saw Neeka, they giddily pulled her out into the hallway.

She looked bewildered. "What's happening? Are Payton and George finally a couple?" she asked.

"No!" Payton said firmly. "But look!" She handed her a brochure.

Neeka seemed just as excited as Selina and her, until she got to the last page. Then her face fell.

"What?" Payton asked.

Neeka handed the brochure back, shrugging. "I'm just not sure it's necessary," she said. "I like the camp at the community center. I don't want to spend all week busing back and forth between home and camp."

"That's the best part—it's an overnight camp! Not only do we get to eat, sleep, and breathe volleyball, but we also get a break away from our parents for four whole nights."

Neeka's interest was piqued again, but there was obviously something holding her back. "I don't know. I need to think about it."

Payton didn't understand Neeka's reaction at all. This was her idea. It meant a lot to her to have both Selina and Neeka on her side. Why was her friend pretending that she wasn't interested?

"Neeka, you know we need this if we have any hope of getting to State," Payton uttered. "You said it yourself. We all need new skills. This camp can get us there."

Conflicting emotions bounced around Neeka's face like a firework display. "I said I'll think about it," she said, then stormed back into the library.

"What's her problem?" Selina asked.

Payton shook her head. "I don't know, but knowing Neeka, she won't tell us until she's good and ready."

CHAPTER 15

JV basketball felt very mechanical. Neeka didn't enjoy it as well as she had when Payton and Selina were on the team with her last year. She pushed through the routine it had become, looking forward to the day they were all on the same team together again. She wouldn't give up basketball, but this season just re-enforced her passion and commitment to volleyball.

At least we get to practice in the small gym, Neeka thought. It saved the walk down to the middle school before every practice. The middle school had their own basketball teams to accommodate.

Unexpectedly, at the end of practice, Val ran up to Neeka. She was fuming. "Meet me outside after you change," she demanded.

"Since you asked so nicely..." But Val was already gone.

Neeka changed slowly, taking her time. She wasn't going to let Val think she could push her around. But soon enough, her curiosity got the better of her and she went outside.

"About time," Val snapped. "What do you know about this volleyball camp Payton is trying to recruit everyone into attending?"

Her voice was shrill. It caught the attention of their teammates standing nearby. Neeka grabbed her arm and guided her out of earshot.

"Very little. She approached me, and I told her I'd think about it."

"Because you saw the price tag, didn't you?" Val guessed.

Neeka nodded. "Yeah, it's really expensive. I'm not sure I can afford it."

"Well, I'm certain I can't!"

To her surprise, Val kicked the curb, frustrated. Neeka had never seen her lose her composure like this before. She was usually a prim and proper Southern girl. The popular one. Not the aggressive one. Not like this.

"Is this only about the price tag?" Neeka asked, sensing something deeper.

Val looked away. "I really want to go," she admitted. "That's the worst part. I wish I could go. But *they* flash it around like it's no problem. They never think about *us*. It's cruel, setting something so good in front of someone even though they can't touch it."

They. Rich kids. She didn't need Val to translate. She fully understood, having thought the same thing herself. Sometimes, those with money didn't even think of those without.

The camp was quite expensive, five times the fees they paid for the camp at the community center. Players that usually attended flashy camps like that were from public schools in good areas with programs that were fully funded. Hickory Academy was a private school, but it was run like a business. Nothing came free. They had to pay their own way through most activities, including camp. It was no problem for the rich or sort of rich kids, but it made things complicated for those on scholarships, like her and Val.

"They weren't trying to be inconsiderate," Neeka told her. "They just got really excited, is all. They weren't thinking. It's a good idea. It's just not practical."

Val hunched forward. "I hate it! I want to go so bad. Do you think they'll go without us?"

Neeka hadn't considered it. "I'm not sure."

"I'd be devastated if they did," Val asserted.

Despite herself, Neeka was pleased Val was so upset. It meant the girl was a lot more committed than she'd let on during the JV volleyball season. That was a good sign for next year.

"You really want to go, don't you?"

Val scowled. "Obviously. That's what I just said."

Neeka didn't take her mood personally. She knew who Val was really mad at—the system. Once again, she was facing what she considered an injustice. *They* got to go to an expensive camp. She and the other few volleyball girls on a scholarship would be limited to the community center camp.

This time, Neeka agreed with her.

It wasn't fair.

****

As the end of the week approached, an anger brewed within Neeka. The more she thought about the volleyball camp, the angrier she became. She could understand why Payton and Selina had been so eager, but what about Coach Mike? He was an adult. He knew about finance. And he certainly knew there were students on the team attending Hickory Academy on scholarship. When he gave Payton his blessing to ask around, why didn't he consider the students who couldn't afford the camp?

She couldn't go to her parents with the issue. Her ma would only call Coach Mike and give him a piece of her mind. And Coach Gina might report everything Neeka said back to him, thinking she was doing good. There was only one person she knew to talk to.

Might as well change the sign from Biology to Guidance Counselor, Neeka mulled as she pushed open the door to the biology lab.

Embarrassed, she found a boy sitting at a table, obviously in the middle of a test.

Saying nothing, Dr. B signaled for her to step back out. He followed behind her, making sure the door was closed tightly behind them.

"Make-up exam," he explained. "He was absent yesterday when I administered it."

"Sorry, I didn't know," Neeka apologized.

Dr. B seemed perplexed by this. "Nor could you. How can I help you?"

Neeka looked around. The hallway was empty. The rest of her classmates were at lunch. But she hated bringing up money issues in general, especially in somewhere public like a hallway. Coach Mike could walk around the corner at any time. Still, she had little choice. She had to get the issue with volleyball camp off her mind.

"I need your advice."

"Yes, I assumed as much," he said.

"Hickory Academy is a great school. Though we all come from different backgrounds, we are, for the most part, treated equally. By the teachers, at least. The other students don't always understand that some of us, those on scholarship, can't afford the same things they can."

Adjusting his glassed, Dr. B looked concerned. "You believe there is some discrimination here against those on a scholarship?"

"Yes," she said truthfully. "Among the students. It usually occurs outside school hours. Sometimes, scholarship students are invited to restaurants they can't afford, or parents won't let their kid 'slum' it at a friend's house—"

"That's awful," Dr. B interrupted. He didn't show much emotion in his voice, but Neeka thought she heard a hint of outrage.

"Trust me, I know. Parents you can't control, but when that discrimination happens in school, it's extra infuriating."

Dr. B nodded his understanding. "So tell me, in what way were you recently discriminated against?"

"Maybe discriminated is too strong of a word. It's more like overlooked. Payton has led this campaign to get all the girls to go to some fancy volleyball camp at a university instead of the community center. And Coach Mike has essentially given her the green light. It's a good idea, in theory, but the reality is that not all of us can afford it."

She paused, forming her thoughts. "It's not just me. Compared to others, I'm in a pretty comfortable situation. My parents both make a decent, middle-income wage. I live in a nice housing estate. My brother drives a used jeep. I'll have a car soon too. Used, of course. But Val's mom is raising her single-handedly. She lives in a tiny house. How could Coach Mike have missed that when he gave his blessing? I mean, some of the parents have to make sacrifices for us to be here."

Dr. B considered her situation. "Have you discussed this with Payton yet?"

"No," Neeka admitted.

"Why is that?"

"This was her idea. She's so excited. I don't want to bring her down. But I need to bring the subject up with someone."

Dr. B quickly popped his head into the classroom to make sure the boy wasn't cheating off his notes. Satisfied, he returned to her. "I don't deny this is tricky. Will the other girls attend the camp, even if the whole team can't?"

"Val wondered the same thing. I don't know."

"Let me rephrase. How would you feel if they did?"

The frown that appeared on her face revealed her true emotions. "I would hate it if that happened. Not only would those left behind feel left out, but it would ruin all efforts Team Scary Pancake made this year to unite the team. This would be yet another divide. We've had enough divides these last two seasons. But..."

She couldn't believe she was about to say this. "But I can't deny the benefit it would be to our overall skill level. Payton was right when she said we need this camp if we have any hope of winning State."

"Well, I think one thing is very clear in all of this. You have every right to turn down Payton's idea, but you must explain why. They won't know unless you tell them. Teach. If you don't, the result could be the divide you're trying to avoid."

Turning to her other source of guidance, Neeka ran upstairs to her room and pulled out *Diary of a Young Volleyball Star* the minute she got home from school. Moving her large yellow comforter to her bay window, along with most of her pillows, she made herself snug as a bug in a rug before opening the book. She was at the very end.

I've decided to go pro, but I doubt I'll last very long. I'm doing it temporarily for the money. My fiancé and I want to build a life together soon, so we have to start saving. My trust fund won't last forever. I'm excited. It'll be a new experience. I've never been one to turn down a challenge. It'll be sad leaving the afterschool program behind, though. I've been tutoring there for years now. And I owe them so much. It's where I met the man of my dreams. They threw us the best engagement party! The kids were so cute. But life only moves forward. So I have to as well.

Speaking of life moving forward... As college comes to a close, and I fill up the last few pages of you, diary, I feel I would be doing Courtney an injustice if I didn't finally talk about what happened to her. I've been avoiding doing so because I didn't want to immortalize it into words. I wanted to pretend it never happened. But it did happened. I can't change that. I have to face it, no matter how ugly and grown-up it is. I lost a friend. She deserves to walk these pages.

Last year, near the midterm break of our first semester, Courtney passed away from heart failure caused by her eating disorder. I thought she had recovered. After the vile comment Coach Leech made freshman year, she got scarily thin, to the point she was put in hospital. Once she was there, the hospital oversaw her recovery. She stayed there the entire summer between freshman and sophomore year. By the time she left, she looked so healthy again! She was still quite thin, more so than she should have been, but color had returned to her cheeks. A renewed energy buzzed within her. She was even able to play volleyball again, made better by the arrival of our new coach.

When we parted ways the summer before junior year, she appeared to be back to her old self, the girl I knew from orientation freshman year. Vibrant and shiny. Then, halfway through the summer, we lost touch. She stopped returning my emails. I just assumed she was busy, so I wasn't too concerned.

Not until I returned to college junior year to find she had dropped out. It wasn't by choice. She was ill again, her body too weak to move for long periods of time. At some point during the summer, she'd relapsed.

I learned all this when I went to visit her at her family's home in upstate New York. I remembered standing outside the large, colonial style house with my suitcase. Red autumn leaves fell around me. I was afraid to go in. From what her parents had said to me on the phone, I think part of me knew it would be the last time I saw her.

Her sister escorted me up to her bedroom. Courtney was surprised to see me when I walked into her room, but I could tell she didn't have much energy to get emotional about it. Her eyes were dull, like she'd given up. Without saying much, I crawled into bed next to her and gave her a big hug. Even then, her heartbeat felt weak against my own.

The next morning, she handed me a necklace with a small gold sun on it, telling me it reminded her of me. I'm assuming she meant because of my last name. Solis. I didn't want to accept it, knowing it was a goodbye present. But I had to. Immediately, I fastened it around my neck and swore never to take it off.

A month later, I returned to New York for Courtney's funeral. I can't say I knew her long, only since freshman year, but when you play on a team, you bond with those around you in a way you don't with most people. Everything is magnified. You become friends quicker, argue more frequently, and laugh in a way that changes you.

Along with her memory, Courtney's necklace will serve as a reminder of so many things. That winning isn't everything. That life is short. That young people are impressionable. In the future, when I coach, I'll stay true to my own values. I'll create a safe, positive environment for my players, a nourishing one where they get to grow, laugh, and prosper, no matter what the scoreboard says. I'll be their protector. Because that's what volleyball has done for me. It's been my shield through the roughest of times, a bit of sunlight in my darkest hours. And my joy when life is good.

The next day, Neeka called a Team Scary Pancake meeting with Coach Mike in his office. He stood by the wall, looking more tired than usual. With volleyball season over, the school had thrown extra responsibilities on his plate. Reading through the hundred sticky notes he had posted around his office, most in neon colors, she realized that a lot of Coach Mike's intensity wasn't because he commanded authority, though he did. It was because he cared. A lot. Even now, he had a legion of ideas for his creative writing class floating around the office, ideas he'd obviously put a lot of time and attention into.

Payton leaned against the whiteboard, smearing one such idea, while Selina was very happily sitting in Coach Mike's favorite chair, spinning around.

"You break my chair, Cho, you wash my car," he warned.

When they looked at her to start the meeting, Neeka felt the anger she'd been carrying around all week surface. She had tried to suppress it, especially before speaking, but when it caught in her throat, refusing to go away, she decided it was better to let it out. Bit by bit, she was learning it was necessary at times to call on her inner Annette, but only now and again, when appropriate. This was one of those occasions.

"Wow, you haven't even said anything yet, and I can tell you're already boiling," Payton said.

Her friend knew her well.

"Why so upset?"

"Camp," she clipped.

"Of course," Selina whined. "The best idea we've had all season, and you're going to sabotage it."

Payton raised her eyebrow at the girl. "We?"

Selina ignored her.

"Neeka's talking," Coach Mike said.

Neeka steadied herself. "Did it not occur to a single one of you that some of the volleyball players can't afford this camp?"

"No," Selina said bluntly, with absolutely no remorse.

Payton looked horrified. "I never even considered that! I'm so sorry, Neeka."

Coach Mike stood back, letting the girls work it out themselves. Neeka was glad. She'd been afraid he'd lash out at her. She had, after all, just scolded him—Coach Mike, the captain of captains.

"Well, you have to keep that in mind when you're making plans. Some players want to go but can't. Now they're really upset."

"Really?" Selina asked. This time, she looked down, embarrassed. "I didn't think anyone would be upset."

"That's the problem. No one was thinking. How would you feel if you were taken to a candy store but told you couldn't eat anything?"

"I'd put as much candy into my mouth as would fit," Selina answered, smiling.

Neeka wasn't amused. "This is serious, Selina."

"Not really," she said, returning to her nonchalant attitude.

Coach Mike decided to step forward, preventing an argument. "I apologize, Neeka. I didn't even think about the issues the cost of the camp would cause. What would you girls like to do?"

"The answer is simple. We don't go," Payton said firmly. "We're a team. If one can't go, none will."

Her anger disappearing, Neeka was thankful to Payton for saying so. Now that the issue was resolved, she felt the same disappointment she read on Payton and Coach Mike's faces. It really had been a good idea. It was probably their only hope of getting to State. Now, that dream slowly started to fade before her.

Selina, however, seemed totally unaffected. She spun around in the chair, a smile haunting her lips.

"Selina?" Neeka asked.

"How am I the only person who sees the solution? Really?" she asked, boastful. "You guys sure gave up pretty easy..."

"Spit it out," Coach Mike instructed her, though by his pleased smile, Neeka suspected he'd figured out what Selina was about to say.

"I don't see why we can't raise the money. Camp ain't until summer. We have plenty of time."

Neeka and Payton looked at each other enthusiastically. "You're a genius!" they said in unison.

"I know." Selina beamed.

CHAPTER 16

"Burgers are the best," Payton said, taking a huge bite of her double quarter pounder. Ketchup and pickles slopped everywhere. The other girls—Selina, Neeka, and Lacey—looked at her with disgust, but she didn't care. The problem with being so tall, athletic, and growing was that she was always hungry.

"I thought hot dogs were the best," Neeka reminded her.

Payton took another bite of her burger as her friends looked away. "Well, if this place served hot dogs, I would have ordered one. Or I'd spike it!" She laughed at her own joke, her mouth full. "Get it... If they *served* hot dogs."

Selina groaned. "Remind me to never again choose a fast food restaurant as a meeting place for Team Scary Pancake. Plus one guest," she added, meaning Lacey.

"Honored guest," Neeka also added.

"Always happy to help," Lacey said. "I couldn't resist, not after Payton told me her great idea."

Payton sighed, happy. Her Saturday was turning out to be quite eventful. First, her dad had called to inform her he was taking her on a father-daughter vacation during spring break, but he wouldn't say where. It was a mystery, a fabulous one. And now this meeting, sitting here with her friends. And this burger.

Life was good.

"I don't know how much Payton told you," Neeka said to Lacey.

"Everything," Payton said, but with her mouth packed with burger, no one understood her.

Neeka continued. "I'm not going to pretend I heard what cave girl just said. Essentially, we want to go to the Jackson University Volleyball Camp, but not everyone can afford it. So we have to have a fundraiser. We were hoping the seniors would participate. We really need all the help we can get."

"Is this why you bought me a mega milkshake? Trying to sweeten me up?" Lacey asked playfully.

Payton nodded proudly. "My idea."

"Well," Lacey said, "I can only speak on my own behalf. I'd love help out. And I'll definitely talk to the rest of the senior girls to see what they say. What kind of fundraiser are y'all thinking about doing?"

"We haven't decided yet," Neeka said. "It's better we make it a team decision. We asked the other girls to meet us in the cafeteria after school on Monday. We were hoping the seniors would be there too."

"Gotcha. I'll make a few phone calls tonight."

"You don't think they'll really help, do you?" Selina asked, picking at a curly fry. "I mean, the season is technically over. You guys now all belong to whatever college team you're going off to."

Lacey seemed disappointed at her words. "Selina, we are still a team. We always will be. A team photo doesn't disappear overnight. It hangs up for eternity."

"Or until a tornado blows it away," she joked, but ate her curly fry happily.

This was great news. With the seniors, Payton was sure they'd definitely come up with a great idea to bring in some dough. She was still embarrassed she hadn't considered Neeka's financial situation when she'd given Coach Mike the material about the camp. She felt she'd failed her as a friend. But watching Selina, Neeka, and Lacey talk about possible fundraiser ideas they could propose to the team to get the ball rolling, it looked as though things were working out okay.

Everything does, in the end. Her dad had told her that, and she believed it.

At their meeting on Monday, the rest of the volleyball team were just as excited about the fundraiser as Team Scary Pancake. Plus one honored guest. They gathered around a table, seniors included, making notes as they brainstormed possible fundraisers.

"Ugg, no car washes or bake sales," Selina stipulated, examining the lists. "It's so unoriginal. No one will want to fork over the cash. We need buckets full. Not just a few measly tin cans."

"I agree. We need something spectacular," Janette said.

"We can challenge the boys' soccer team to a match and charge admission," a senior suggested. "You know, a whole girl power thing. We can beat the boys."

"I'm not sure Coach Gina would go for it," Lacey said. "It's a sore subject with her that Hickory Academy hasn't yet introduced a boys' volleyball team. I think she wants her son to play. Best not to highlight the fact."

Payton listened as those around her continued to shout out ideas. They were all good ideas, except for Selina's poker idea to count cards at a casino, but they all had their downfalls. There were either too many upfront costs involved, or the income they'd likely make wouldn't be enough to cover all the team's camp fees. So that no one felt singled out, they'd make it a goal to come up with an idea that could pay for the entire team to go, not just those who couldn't afford it.

Eventually, Val, who had been abnormally quiet, raised her hand. "You know, there are companies that help schools with fundraising. They give you catalogs to sell things like shirts, accessories, candy, and food—things that please teachers, parents, and students."

"I don't know," Payton said. "The karaoke club did something like that during the holidays."

"And table tennis sold magazine subscriptions," a sophomore added.

Val didn't budge. "Yes, but how we sell our goods can be original. Like we can get permission to dress up like werewolves and vampires and advertise 'monster' deals when we ask people to buy stuff. Some gimmick that will catch their attention."

This caught Payton's attention. It was actually a really good idea. If they made it fun, people wouldn't mind spending money. It'd be memorable and worthy!

"I'm sold," she said.

The rest of the team agreed with her, excited. They thought it was a fab idea and congratulated Val for coming up with it. As they started throwing out ideas for what gimmick they'd use, Payton was delighted to see the freshmen girls were finally starting to act like part of the team.

"We need something the school will respond to," Janette said.

Lacey came up with the winning idea.

"Let's wear T-shirts with an image of a cactus in the center. We can then promise that next year's volleyball team will take Big Joe with them to camp and post photos from everywhere they go. Y'all can squeeze him onto the bus, into your dorm, in the lunch line. You might even convince the instructors to let you take a photo of him with you gals on the court."

"Big Joe is gigantic," Neeka protested. "We'll never fit him anywhere."

"Don't knock it just yet," a junior said. "I remember the Back to the Alamo Day. There was also a smaller version of Big Joe being tossed across the halls, sunglasses and all, but the football team accidently popped him when they were messing around."

"Ah, yes, the notorious Little Joe," another junior giggled. "Poor guy. He's probably lying at the bottom of a trash can somewhere."

"Or the drama department prop closet," the first junior informed them. "I saw him there at the start of the year when I was looking for ruby slippers."

"Awesomesauce!" Lacey exclaimed. "We can patch up Little Joe and you gals can take him with you to camp and post the photos online."

"The T-shirts can read 'We saved Little Joe. Now save volleyball!'" Courtney recommended.

"Perfect!" Val sat up, as if she was ready to get started there and then. "For added effect, we can wear cowgirl hats. For anyone who doesn't have one of her own, they sell them at the dollar store."

Courtney looked confused. "For anyone who doesn't have one of their own?" she quoted. "Why would you assume anybody here would have—" She stopped herself, realizing her mistakes. "Never mind.

Forgot I was in Nashville, not San Francisco."

"Don't let them conform you," Selina objected. "Stick with me, California. We'll lead the rebel cause together."

Payton didn't have a hat either. "Trip to the dollar store?" she asked Neeka.

Neeka smiled. "Sure thing."

As the girls left the cafeteria, their meeting over, Payton ran up to Val. Their relationship was strained, given everything that had happened with JV. Like Little Joe, she wanted to patch things up. They still had two more years of volleyball and basketball to get through together.

"Think you can outsell me?" she asked lightheartedly, baiting Val into a friendly competition.

Val took no offense by it, as Payton had hoped. She seemed keen. "No, I don't think I can. I know it."

"I doubt it. I'm a year ahead of you, girl. I have connections. Unless, of course, you ask Jamari to take a catalog to his school..."

Val turned red and flinched. The joke clearly didn't sit well with her. Payton felt bad. She wanted to bond with Val, not mortify the girl.

"Sorry, too far," she said.

"It's okay," Val reassured her. "I have my eye on a new guy. Stephen, from the lacrosse team."

"You really go for athletes, don't ya?"

"Yep," Val said.

"Me too," Payton confessed. "But don't worry, not Stephen. He's all yours."

Val shuffled her bag. "That's a relief to hear, because we're already dating!" she laughed.

The fundraiser took a few weeks to organize. Before they did anything else, they had to choose the right company to sell products for, one that gave them a fair deal and appealed to their target customer base—the students. After a long online search at a team sleepover at Payton's house one night, they found a company that had an assortment of funky items. Laptop covers of famous paintings.

Socks that looked like tattoos. Celebrity-inspired perfumes.

They then decided on a week to hold the fundraiser. They'd collect orders for a month in total, but they wanted a week completely dedicated to actively searching out orders. The Hickory Academy administration had refused their idea to dress in full cowgirl gear for the week they selected, but they did give them permission to wear their T-shirts under their blazers and, at lunch only, their cowgirl hats.

Brandon Moore had sprung for the T-shirts. He felt partly responsible for the fundraiser, since camp had been his idea, and wanted to help oversee the project.

"Make sure you send some catalogs up my way. I'm surrounded by a bunch of old geezers with money to burn," he'd said when Payton thanked him for the T-shirts.

"Just give them the link for the website. But make sure you give them the school reference number to type into the checkout. That's the only way we get credited with the order. The company we're using also has an app for purchases, if it makes it easier."

"Baby girl, what part of 'old geezers' did you not understand? I barely know what an app is. Better send the catalogs up."

"Fine," Payton agreed. "I'll have mom mail them tomorrow."

"What's the next step, now that you've set a date and have the T-shirts and catalogs?" he asked.

"We're printing out labels with details to the Instagram page we set up," Payton answered. "That's the whole gimmick—if we earn enough to go to volleyball camp, the students get to see one of our most beloved mascots travel around with us. It'll be hilarious!"

Little Joe had been safely rescued from the drama department during a secret mission where Selina finally got to embrace her Agent Cho side. The first photo of Little Joe was already uploaded. He relaxed in a hammock-style stand surrounded by volleyballs. A caption read: *Follow volleyball this summer. See what Little Joe gets up to next! Fund his trip!*

"I'm assuming you're going to stick the labels on the catalogs," her dad reckoned.

"Precisely."

He sounded pleased. "Well done to you and the volleyball girls.

Don't worry, I'll make sure you gals get to camp. Even if I have to buy every last tattoo sock myself!"

The week of the fundraiser arrived. Between setting an account up with the company, waiting for catalogs to come through the mail, and making sure they had enough time to prepare, the team had decided to hold the fundraiser in early April. Pulling her T-shirt over her head before school that Monday morning, Payton realized with a heavy heart that the school year was almost over. In a few months, Lacey would no longer walk the hallways. And Jamari would move away from home, leaving his orange jeep with Neeka.

"We'll be fine," Neeka had assured her, though she also sounded sad when Payton had brought it up the night before.

After her mom dropped her off, Payton ran inside to meet up with her teammates in the cafeteria. They all grinned at each other in their glittering cactus T-shirts. Almost as if watching over them, Big Joe stood strong and tall in the corner of the room, recently re-inflated. Lacey was the last to join them, hauling a majority of the catalogs in from her car.

"Ready?" she asked them brightly.

They all cheered.

"Then let's get this rodeo started!"

The girls planned to spend the week pleading with their fellow classmates. They'd each memorized a speech about how the money was to help the team improve, get to the next level. They wanted to stress the benefits of the camp so that the students understood they weren't just being picky about where they went. They really needed the instruction the Jackson University Volleyball Camp provided.

But it wasn't necessary.

The students were more than eager to order from the company, and not just because of the cool gadgets. They just wanted to help the team.

"Of course!" they said to Payton time after time. "We love volleyball."

"Sell the T-shirts too! We all want one with Little Joe on it!"

Midweek, of the boys grabbed her hat off her head at lunch. "I'll pay you for a kiss!" he'd teased.

"Keep the hat!" she'd countered. "But make sure you put two dollars in the pot!"

The pot was a collection jar the students had started on their own initiative, in the form of an upside down cowgirl hat, which was under Dr. B's care in the biology lab. Those who couldn't afford to make a purchase and those who simply weren't interested in any of products had started donating cash instead, and the trend spread.

By the end of the week, things were looking good for volleyball camp. According to the daily status report the company sent, online sales alone had exceeded the girls' expectations. It would be awhile before they got the results of the catalog sales, and the fundraiser wasn't finished yet, they would continue to accept orders trickling in over the next few weeks, but Payton was almost certain they'd raised enough money to pay for all their camp fees.

"Thank goodness it's Friday. I can't believe everyone bought so much!" Neeka said, meeting Payton at her locker. "I'm exhausted. George alone bought fifty dollars worth of chocolates from me. I hope they don't melt in the mail."

"Really?" Payton asked. "I still haven't seen him around. I think he's avoiding me."

"Maybe the chocolate is to cure his heartache after you rejected him," Neeka kidded.

Payton felt bad. "I didn't reject him. I just never accepted him. Not yet," she said.

Neeka's eyes went big. "Not yet?" she squeaked.

"Whatever," Payton mumbled. "We'll see. I don't know." She shook her head. "Anyway, it doesn't matter right now. We're going to the Jackson University Volleyball Camp!"

"I don't know why you're acting so surprised," Selina said, coming up behind them. "Look at all the support we received this year. The cheering after Sub-State even though we lost? They love us! We gave them an undefeated season. It's the first undefeated season Hickory Academy has had, in any sport, since the 1980s."

"Really?" Neeka asked in surprise. "I didn't know that."

Payton had. Her dad had pointed it out to her a million times. He knew Hickory Academy's history well. He'd been a student at the school himself, years and years and years ago.

Payton took it all in. The undefeated season. The support from their fans. The success of the fundraiser. The future of the Hickory Academy volleyball program was no longer a team effort. It now involved the whole school.

We helped do this, she reflected proudly, watching as Selina and Neeka tried to spray water on each other in celebration of all they had accomplished.

I guess we're pretty good leaders after all.

****

A few days into May, the final numbers for the fundraiser came in. The volleyball team had earned enough to pay for camp, with some in the pot for the following year. The numbers were no surprise, not after hearing reports from other girls on the team. But it meant they could soon officially register for the camp.

To congratulate the girls, Coach Mike and Coach Gina pitched in to host an After-Fundraiser party at the local skating rink. Under the flashing lights of the disco ball, with Neeka trying to not fall flat on her face next to her, Payton thought forward to the coming year.

"We've really grown as a team," she said.

Neeka stumbled in response. "Can't talk. Skating."

Payton laughed. "If you keep holding your arms forward, you're just going to stay off balance. Relax into it. Trust your legs."

"Easy for you to say." She blew her cheeks out, concentrating as she dropped her arms. "What were you saying?"

"We've grown a lot as a team. Think how far we've come in only two years. I think it's a good sign. I really feel we can make it to State next year and win."

Neeka waited until they rounded the top of the rink before speaking. "I want to agree, it's a great goal to set, but I also don't want to get overconfident. Not after seeing the way Cumberland Lake performed. Let's just get through camp first. Then we can talk about team goals."

Payton knew Neeka was right, but she didn't want to listen. Not on a night such as this, with the other volleyball girls chatting over nachos and laughing as they skated to their favorite hits on the radio. There was too much hope and happiness in the air. There was so much potential.

The fundraiser had been a success because their school believed in them. She wouldn't let her classmates down. Be it as a leader or a starting player, she would get Hickory Academy to State next year. Of that, she was certain.

She sent a mental warning out to all the other volleyball teams they might come up against next season.

I hope you all are ready for Hickory Academy. Because you're about to be served a slice of You've Just Been Creamed pie.

ABOUT THE AUTHOR

Pam comes from a long line of volleyball lovers, including her four brothers who all played for their college teams and her father who was a coach. Pam has spent the past two years travelling as a physical therapist with a beach volleyball competition circuit. She figures what better way to semi-retire than to travel from one beach to another, watching the sport she loves. In her spare time she is an avid snorkeler and she loves kayaking and walking the beach with her husband of almost 20 years.

CPSIA information can be obtained
at www.ICGtesting.com
Printed in the USA
LVOW04s2303060616

491490LV00029B/925/P